SNEAK TEACHING

Grant Pylkas

Sneak Teaching
Copyright © 2005 by Grant Pylkas
All rights reserved.

No part of this book may be used or reproduced in any manner without written permission except for brief quotations used in reviews and critiques.

The characters in this fictional work are the product of my imagination and any likeness to any real individual is coincidence.

Cover design and layout by
Yvonne Vermillion, Magic Graphix.

Editing in the preparation of this book by
Chuck Vermillion, Help Publish.

Printed in the United States of America.

Published by
BookShelf Press
Livermore, CA
www.bookshelfpress.com

The Bookshelf® name, logo and colophon are the trademarks of WingSpan Publishing.

ISBN 1-59594-019-7
EAN 978-1-59594-019-3
First Edition 2005

Library of Congress Control Number: 2005928646

Dedication

This book is dedicated to Elizabeth Ostrowski, my niece, who at the age of sixteen ended her addiction to drugs and joined The Ancestors. It is in her memory that I wrote this book.

This book is also dedicated to many young relatives who walked into a recovery center and started a new life.

I need to make mention of a young man who's daily recovery is of special importance. Alex Hennessey was almost lost to all of us who understand this disease called addiction. We thought that he was about to join The Ancestors. He didn't; he walked though those scary doors of recovery and is the promise of AA come true, alive, and recovering today.

This book is for all who take the scary walk though that door and into their first AA meeting. They all are the proof that the promises of AA come true, one day at a time.

Acknowledgements

I would like to thank Leila Whittinger of Education Minnesota for her help in reviewing the content of the book for errors and her insight into the workings of Union contracts.

I would also like to thank Dick Grossman for his input and encouragement.

Contents

Chapter 1	Jeffery Canna	1
Chapter 2	One Mad "She Bear"	11
Chapter 3	Pay Back	17
Chapter 4	"Jeffery Canna Lives"	28
Chapter 5	Dr. Fritz	35
Chapter 6	"The Old Hand Speaks"	40
Chapter 7	"Epiphany"	47
Chapter 8	"Real Teaching"	52
Chapter 9	ZJ	59
Chapter 10	First Day	64
Chapter 11	A Tale of Two Students	70
Chapter 12	The Set Up	80
Chapter 13	The Accusation	85
Chapter 14	The Deal	90
Chapter 15	Big Guy	95
Chapter 16	The Cave	102
Chapter 17	The Sting	108
Chapter 18	Hockey Hank	114
Chapter 19	Impulse	120
Chapter 20	Reprisal	127
Chapter 21	Drugs Inc.	133
Chapter 22	Pyrrhic Victory	138
Chapter 23	Who Let the Dogs Out?	143
Chapter 24	Gameboy	149
Chapter 25	The Big Lie	155
Chapter 26	Compromise, I Think?	166
Chapter 27	Game Plan	171
Chapter 28	A Walk in the Parking Lot	183
Chapter 29	The Deed	190
Chapter 30	Letting Go	197
Chapter 31	Resurrection	200
Chapter 32	The Rose	206
Chapter 33	Goal	213
Chapter 34	Principal Canna, Roll Over	223

Chapter 1

Jeffery Canna

I was a "Hood," destined for jail and then Hell. I was told, in no uncertain terms, that Hell was waiting and that jail would be no better. Jail was just the jumping off place for Hell, and I was a sure bet for both. An aging, raging busybody took up that bet in the winter of 1960.

My name is "P" —— a nickname that the family gave me. It sticks to this day. I'm the guy that this fanatic was making predictions about and condemning to Hell. It is me, "P".

In 1959, my family moved from the city of St. Paul, Minnesota, and into South St. Paul, a suburb where my father worked. I was transplanted from a small neighborhood school in St. Paul, to an over-crowded, suburban school with large classes and teachers that were in their fifties and sixties. Like many other baby-boomers, I was born three years after World War II and just before the Korean War. I was nine years old and young for the fourth grade. I was so skinny that my ribs showed through my chest. I wasn't tall, but I wasn't short, either. My hair was in a very short, almost shaved cut called a "Heinie" in those days.

I was already behind in my studies when I moved to my new school, having been sick at home with swollen tonsils during most of the first half of the school year. Frankly, I did not want to leave my fourth-grade friends or my teacher at Como Elementary School. I was happy at that school. I had been the happiest I was to be for some time in the near future.

I also had to move into a smaller bedroom with my older, seventh-grade brother. The room was far too small for two boys of any age. We had shared a large attic bedroom in the old house, and we'd had lots of room. It didn't matter that I liked my brother and had real respect for him. I just didn't want to live in the same room with him. We fought a lot in the new place.

We moved, celebrated Christmas and the New Year holidays, and then off to school I went.

It was as cold as the Artic on the first day I went to South Saint Paul's Lincoln Elementary School. It was a sunny and crisp twenty-seven degrees below zero on that morning, a temperature that can freeze human skin in about a minute. Fortunately, our car was parked in a garage attached to our new house, unlike the garage at our previous house on Grotto Street in St. Paul. Starting our car in our old place was always a gamble. Would it start, or would it be frozen? At that time, having a warm garage provided an elevated social status.

The day she delivered me to Lincoln School, Mom told me what was on her mind. She gave a little speech, "We have moved up. The family has experienced a social transformation from poor inner city kids to the next generation of professional adults. You will all become the adults I expect you to become. You are special, with talents that belong only to you. You will discover those talents and become someone that will make me and your dad proud."

Mom believed that her children would make it. She believed that we, all five of us, would go to college and become doctors, lawyers, or teachers. She was not afraid to believe in each and every one of us.

So it was that she delivered me to Lincoln Grade School in South St. Paul on that cold, sunny day in 1960. She came with an optimistic attitude and an open willingness to do what had to be done to achieve the status that her children deserved. We walked up cement stairs onto an outdoor landing, and then through double wooden doors onto another landing at the bottom of more stairs. We climbed the creaky wooden stairs to the third floor, turned right, and then entered a door bearing gold letters, bordered in black that read, OFFICE. We stood before a counter where the secretary's desk separated us from an inner office. Neatly painted block letters that read, JEFFERY CANNA, PRINCIPAL, were on the wooden door's frosted window glass.

The secretary told Mom, "The principal wants to see you." So we sat down and waited for about an hour for him to see us. The paperwork had been done earlier, but Mom didn't say anything because she was raised to be nice.

The principal of Lincoln School was at least sixty years old, fat, and gray haired. The middle of his head was balding, he was shaped like a pear, and he was very set in his ways. Jeffery Canna had probably been educated in the early twenties. He told us that he had attended a private college and had earned a liberal arts degree. He had no idea what educational research was, or how any educational training worked, for that matter. He didn't need to know how any such nonsense worked. He could care less anyway, since his staff was about the same age as he, and of the same educational era. "Drill, drill, drill, and more drill was the only thing you have to know to be in this teaching game," said Principal Canna.

He had to be the personification of every schoolchild's worst nightmare. He was scary to me. I can remember feeling all jittery while waiting to see him. Even though she should have been afraid of him, Mom wasn't scared. Mom was an eternal optimist. Principal Canna was of the old school, believing that to "Spare the rod" was to "Spoil the child." He was not afraid to tell us this. He cared little for complaining mothers, and even less for complaining mothers from foreign places. In fact, anyone who came from anywhere other than South St. Paul was foreign to him. We would soon find out how that attitude was to change our lives. He would act on his understandings of this lady and her kid.

The world for Jeffery Canna was Lincoln school, where he had been the principal for only a short time. Considering the shorter life expectancy at that time, he had become "The Boss" at an advanced age. It was about time, in his estimation, that he was chosen to be the principal. He had paid all the dues for the position, by teaching, serving as assistant principal, and now, at sixty, he was principal.

He was a condescending bully. He believed that students and children were to be controlled. I was yet to learn that lesson the hard way. The following course of events influenced nearly every decision I've made during my lifetime. I just hope that no child ever has to experience what I endured during that winter of 1960.

I was a newcomer to Jeffery Canna's Lincoln School. It really was "Jeffrey Canna's Lincoln School." Canna was in possession of that school, as well as my "Ass." He behaved towards me as if I were an unclean and unwashed street "Hood" needing to be taught discipline. He thought for sure I was preordained to work in some menial job in the lowest place in society. I was from St. Paul Public Schools where the students were socially promoted and traditional academic standards were, according to Canna, "Not strictly followed."

The inner city schools were, in those days, some of the most progressive in the country, especially in St. Paul. The University Of Minnesota School Of Education was revered in the St. Paul school system, and its graduates were coveted in its classrooms. In those days, most of St. Paul's schoolteachers were from the University of Minnesota. Canna's staff came from private schools of high regard, in his estimation.

Canna's opinion of us was also tainted because my dad worked for a "Communist organization," the Farmers Union Central Exchange. It's known today as Cennex Harvest States, a fortune 500 company. At this time, Senator Joe McCarthy was not yet history, nor were healed the wounds caused by the House Un-American Committee's allegations. "Commies" were everywhere, including agricultural cooperatives that competed with "For profit" businesses.

The atmosphere in the early sixties, in Minnesota, was replete with fear and "Red baiting," especially amongst the conservative right. This was also true of the meat packers of South St. Paul. While the meat packers union wasn't a right wing conservative organization, it didn't care for communists.

In this uneducated, blue-collar suburb, where unions were the saviors of the general population, the meat packing plants gave good jobs to Americans of Serbian, Croatian, Polish, and Italian heritage. The workers shared a culture of patriotism that was fostered by the union bosses. The communists had killed their sons in Korea, and anyone accused of being a "Commie" felt the sting of hatred and bias that was previously directed at people of other races. A lot of the union workers also hated blacks, homosexuals, Jews, and Asians. Some of them seemed to hate everyone, except for themselves of course. The reality was that they didn't always get along real well with each other, either

My dad would say, "Thank God, I'm just 'Pink' because of my employment choice." He worked for a farmer's cooperative which concentrated the buying power of many farmers into a group that could buy large quantities of agricultural support products at attractive prices. Co-op was a dirty word in 1960, as a co-op was linked, by the uneducated, to the Russian collective farms that were part of a centralized economy of Communist Russia.

My dad would state with some disdain, "The reality is that the farmers union is not pink or red. Nothing could be further from the truth." Yet, the general public of South Saint Paul saw the cooperative as a communist plot to subvert the "For profit" business community by cutting out part of the distribution system. Worse yet, the farm group cooperated on the sale and distribution of the field and dairy produce grown by the member farms. Dad would tell Mom, "The meatpackers think the Farmers Union Co-operative is just a step away from packing its own meat, and that would be a real threat to the union worker on the floor of the largest packing plants in the world, the home of Swift and Armors Meat Packing."

Dad had the feeling that the gap of misunderstanding had more to do with the unions thinking they were better than everyone else than it had to do with any real threats that the co-op might pose. He once told me, "The Farmers Union members are crop farmers with no interest in being in the meat packing business. They are more interested in being in the oil business than competing with the well established, low profit meat businesses." He would turn out to be right.

Ironically, in their own eyes, unions weren't "Commie" organizations. Only cooperatives were "Commie" organizations. The close relationship between the unions and the Communist Party during the depression years was conveniently forgotten. A critical understanding of history, especially their own, was not important to the rank and file union workers. They maintained their high standard of living because they believed in "God and Country" and whatever the union bosses said. If the union bosses hated the Farmers Union Central Exchange and all it represented, then so did they.

The farmers for whom my father worked couldn't have been further from being communists. They were independent "Sons of bitches" with nothing but a profit motive in mind. They gathered together to form a buying group for one reason: To increase their own profits. If this was communism, then General Electric must have been communist, also.

Well, ol' Jeffery Canna picked up on the community theme of using the label of "Commies" for Farmers Union workers. Jeffery was also probably jealous of the fact that Farmers Union employed mostly white-collar workers in South St. Paul where the cooperative's headquarters were. Canna was not well paid as a public servant, while Dad had been very well paid for an uneducated man. My dad spoke with reverence about the time he spent in Europe. He spoke about the time he spent in the army, and he stated many times, "I was given a unique set of skills. I obtained those skills, and an appreciation for leadership, in General Bradley's World War II Headquarters in London." Dad would go on to say, "I am able to move goods efficiently for large organizations, because I had done this for General Bradley's Fifth Army in Europe. This is what I had done in 'The War' and am now doing for the Mid-west farmers." The skill was in demand, and he was paid very well for what the U.S. Army had taught him.

I suspect that this "Paid very well" thing really angered Canna. Canna was college educated in an era when college graduates were rare and was earning very little for his efforts. Along comes this uneducated "Hick" and his brood of "Hoods" living and prospering in his hometown. Mom, however, had not yet figured this out on that cold morning in January as she waited to see Canna. We were to find out how deep that hatred ran, but it would take some time.

Yeah, that was us, the "Commie hoods" from St. Paul, come to put on "Airs" for all. Not only did Dad work for a communist co-op, he was married to an educated, elementary schoolteacher. She was an educated woman and a commie! I'm sure that my liberal mom, educated at the University of Minnesota, presented a threat to an over-the-hill, sixty-year-old principal who was seriously lacking in human relation skills. She was a threat, because Mom knew the education business and good educational practices.

Mom was a small, pretty lady, and well spoken, but on the other hand, she was a force not to be taken lightly. She was perfectly willing to stand up for what she believed was right. I'm sure that my scrappiness today comes from her. I had never seen her in action until that winter of 1960. I think that she had not had a reason to defend her values before this, but I was to find a person in Mom that I didn't recognize. I'm sure glad I got to see that part of Mom. She taught me so much about life and passion during that cold winter.

I was placed in a class that was taught by a sixty-six-year-old German spinster, Miss Lanterland. Educated in 1920, she believed in the "Drill and kill" teaching technique. I didn't get along with her. I didn't like her, and she didn't care. She never asked what I had done at the old school, never asked a personal question, and probably never even knew how old I was. She didn't care; I didn't care. I checked out; my body was there but my mind was elsewhere. I tested, teased, and talked when I wanted and never gave a rip as to what she wanted.

Miss Lanterland would say, "It's one thing to have a child who is willful and dumb, but it's quite a handful to have one that's willful and smart." I was smart, and because of her and Canna, I have been proving how smart I still am. I could always get the class to laugh at me. I could also entice others to misbehave, and I did.

Miss Lanterland would tell my mom, "He's as mean as could be one minute, charming the next, and horrible after that. He doesn't read worth a damn. He can't spell, and he hates math." I learned to hate that year; I mean, really hate, with all my heart. That was a lot for a nine year old to learn.

The poor behavior I exhibited didn't last very long. No teacher, good or bad, will put up with that type of behavior. I was in the office more than in the classroom. It was nothing for me to be grabbed by the arm, dragged down the hall, and literally thrown into a chair in the principal's office. I confirmed every label that ol' Jeffery Canna applied to me. Canna told me, "You are a hood, destined for jail and then Hell." I was also told in no uncertain terms, "Hell is waiting, and jail will be no better. Jail is just the jumping off place for Hell, and you are a sure bet for both."

By the time I reached home on most days, I thought that jail and Hell were sounding pretty good. Of course, Dad didn't believe a thing I said. Mom was more understanding but not very pleased. It took a lot to get Mom pissed off, but I was trying and it was working. I really thought she would send me back to that Como school in St. Paul where the teacher knew me, and, I was sure, loved me. If I could keep this up, we might even move back to our old house on Grotto Street. I believed this. I really did! I could fool myself, back then. Sometimes I wondered how different my life might have been if we had never moved. We did move, however, and that leads us to the rest of my story.

Chapter 2

One Mad "She Bear"

Mom graduated from the University of Minnesota in 1942 after finishing her training in elementary education. This was a real feat for a depression-era child of a postman. During the war, however, Mom worked at a bank where she could earn more money than as a teacher. She waited for Dad to come home so they could start a family and start living again.

In 1946, Dad came home from World War II and went directly to work for the Farmers Union Central Exchange. Like a lot of other guys who made it home alive, Dad would say, "I'm one lucky son-of-a bitch."

The U.S. Army taught him skills he could use in the peacetime, private sector which made up for his lack of a formal education.

Dad was legally blind if not wearing corrective lenses, making him unfit for combat, but he had still been capable of other safer duties. Better yet, he had made high scores on his army enlistment aptitude test. As a result, he spent his war years coordinating the shipment of war materials from the U.S. to the war zones. He was a Master Sergeant by the time he got out in 1946, and he used those skills again when he served in Korea in 1950. He loved the army, and the army loved him.

The Farmers Union loved him, as well. He had

skills mostly possessed only by college graduates. They didn't have to pay him as well as a college guy, therefore, they loved him.

Mom and Dad were married in 1946. My brother David was born in 1947, and I was born in 1949. Gail arrived in 1951, Diane in 1952, and Bruce came along in 1960, the same year we moved. The year I became the "Child from Hell."

"What a mess," my mother would say. "A new baby at home and a big baby in the fourth grade." I didn't help matters any for her. I wanted to go back to our house on Grotto Street, the old house. I devoted every effort, and every thought, to making life miserable at home as well as at school. As things became worse, the better the past looked to me.

This wasn't done without my paying a price for it. Believe me! It came at great physical expense. I spent many hours doing hated chores at home, and I took my share of hits to the back of the head at school. At school, the worst of the physical violence was yet to come. It was Canna's version of, "I'll pick you up by the ear, drag you out of the room, grab an arm, and pick you up off the ground," routine. These were the actual words he would use, and I remember them as both humiliating and painful. I was small enough so that almost anyone could grab my arm and pick me up off the floor. This seemed to be a favored discipline, since it left no marks but did separate the arm from its socket, and it also hurt like hell.

Even back then, when it was still legal to hit kids in school, the "Dr. Spock" child psychologist generation of parents and teachers believed that striking a child was not the correct thing to do. Canna must not have been reading the good Doctor Spock. The "No marks on the kid" thing worked well for him, since he could honestly inform my parents that he hadn't hit me. This also made me look like a liar to my dad when I told him about the abuse I was receiving at school. Like a true con artist, Canna worked Mom and Dad by dividing them as effectively, and as often, as he could. It worked like a charm.

But the charm's magic finally fizzled out, one day, as Canna dragged me down the hall with my feet barely touching the ground and repeating his litany of favorite phrases, such as, "I'll pick you up by this ear and be careful not to tear it." He would say this just loud enough for me to hear it. Then he would say, "Here comes the arm pull." The final humiliation was the, "Get your ass in the office!"

This day, I'd had it. Before we got to the arm thing, I managed a well-placed kick to the old bastard's balls. He caught all seventy pounds of my anger, causing him to lose his grip on me. He wrenched and doubled over, moaning, and I was sure I'd hurt him. I ran off like a shot, racing down the hall at full speed. I really thought that I could escape.

At nine years old, you just don't get away. I had no more than escaped his reach when a passing teacher appeared out of nowhere and caught me. As she grabbed me, she struck me directly in my face with her open hand. It felt like I'd been hit in the face with a shovel. I was surprised, stunned, and plenty scared. She sure didn't seem to care what happened to me when she delivered me back to Canna. "Here he is, sir," was all she said.

Jeffery Canna was explosive in his anger. He punched me, shoved me, and finally, he lost all reason and became an enraged animal. When one of his assaults soundly connected, I was thrown to the floor. He drew back with his foot and kicked me in the side, as I was sprawled face down on the floor. I remember that I could smell the banana oil used to clean the wooden floors just seconds before I felt the kick. When his kick struck my body, he stopped. He knew the minute his shoe struck me that he had gone too far.

When he stopped, I saw real fear in the old man's eyes for the first time. He might have believed that he had killed me, and I'm sure he could tell that he had severely injured me. I couldn't feel anything, but I knew I was hurt, bad.

I know that I was suspended somewhere, because I didn't know where I was, or worse yet, I didn't know who I was. The violence and pain had created a kind of life force all its own, and within me, it had given birth to a powerful sense of impending doom. I didn't understand it, since I had never experienced such violence. I remember the feeling because it was so vivid.

I felt an intense need to be vindicated, but it was the connection to other living things that felt strongest in me. I was suddenly aware of a connection to Mother Earth, to all living things, and a deep fear inside me. I cannot describe the kind of hatred that was capable of creating this kind of violence towards a helpless child, but I can still recall the chill of dread that I experienced that afternoon.

When Canna stopped his assault I somehow managed to get to my feet, and then I began to run. I must have gotten an adrenaline rush or something. Oddly enough, even as badly as I was hurt, I didn't feel anything during the twenty or so feet I was able to cover before the world all went black.

I regained consciousness in Dr. Shannon's office with Mom's arms around me and with Dad standing behind her. In those days, patients would be first taken to a doctor's office and then only to the hospital if necessary. When Canna realized that I wasn't breathing, he called the police and they called Mom. She had the police take me to the doctor's office. At the doctor's office, she lifted me off the examination table and held my unconscious body in her arms. She really thought that I was dead.

Mom began barking orders at the police, "Get away from my son!"

The local cops, probably protecting Canna's job, did anything that Mom asked. I doubt that they gave a damn what happened to a street kid from St. Paul, but they must have been protecting Canna at the same time. Things were different back then.

Dr. Shannon looked at Mom and said, "I found two broken ribs." He also told her, "He's badly bruised, and I don't know if there are internal injuries." Dr. Shannon was very worried and had no real way of knowing the extent of the beating. I wasn't dead, but I was really beaten up. This was enough to ignite both Mom and Dad. I thought to myself, and then said, "Finally! We can go home to Grotto Street. I'm home free. I can go back to the teachers who liked me and back to my attic in the old house."

I didn't count on the level of anger about to visit me, however. Mom was mad as Hell, at me, at Canna, and at the world. She said, "Why did you disappoint me?" She also hit me with, "I knew you were unhappy, but I never expected you to be so disobedient."

The loud discussions behind Mom and Dad's bedroom door lasted for two days. They were both angry, but Mom was doing most of the yelling. I could hear Dad say, "I want to approach this mess with some degree of level-headedness." But she said, "I want a conference! I want a confrontation!"

As always, Dad lost. He could win the money

arguments, but Mom always won the kid arguments. I think this was probably why their marriage had worked so well for so many years. I'm sure she loved him, but she had a keen instinct about their individual strengths and how to use them. He loved her enough to know the limits of his control. He was also smart enough to know that his educated wife understood some things better than he did.

After I spent three great days at home with tomato soup, "I love Lucy" reruns, and lots of attention, it was time to get on with it. Mom made arrangements for me to return to school, and I had no choice. I finally understood that there was no going back to St. Paul and no returning to the world I loved, and that was that.

I knew she had a plan. She was still mad, and the people in her sights were about to find out just what this little lady with a mission could do. She was one mad she-bear with a wounded cub.

Chapter 3

Pay Back

In today's world, Canna would have been fired. Back in the 1960s, however, he was not only tolerated by the public, but often revered by many as being the strict disciplinarian that it was necessary to be to effectively educate kids. The fact that he had hit a child didn't surprise anyone, nor was the injury life threatening. Therefore, it was an acceptable act. These things occasionally happened in the life of a school principal while doing his job, and back then it was okay, as long as it didn't become a habit. The school board received a report and life moved on for Canna.

I was going to be failed in the fourth grade, Canna had decided, yet I was going to have to finish the year; I just didn't know it yet. This was decided without my mom's knowledge or consent. In fact, she wasn't even informed of this or any other decisions that Canna or the school board had made. All this was done in secret; lots of things were kept secret in those days.

Mom, however, had known for a long time that Canna didn't live in a vacuum. She knew that he would have to deal with his act of violence in some way.

Mom intuitively knew this sixty-year-old principal. She told Dad, "As long as it is just a matter of disagreement about child management style, I will work as best I can with Canna." She was disciplined and careful up to this point. She said to Dad, "The problem now is that this Canna has hit my son, and God knows that's unacceptable."

She went on to say to Dad, "Canna has also been disingenuous with me, committing the sin of omission. He has not been forthcoming about the use of force to gain compliance. Obtaining the desired behavior was his only mission. My son's education was secondary to him, and it didn't even enter his mind. My son was a problem, but violence should not be the answer." She told Dad it was time to act.

The best one of Mom's skills was her ability to see into the future with remarkable accuracy. She was uncanny at predicting human behavior. What she couldn't do was create the right moment to act on her predictions. She would have to wait for that. She had to wait patiently for the circumstance to present itself that would allow an unexpected strike at the enemy.

At this point, it was a fight. She never said it, but Canna was now the object of her thoughts and deeds. All she needed now was an opening or just the appearance of a mistake on the part of Canna. She was now consumed by her need to gain a position from which she could negotiate an outcome she desired.

Mom didn't like doing these things, and Dad wasn't enough of a street fighter to know how. It was left up to Mom to take on Canna. January went by and in February, along with Washington's, Dad's birthday was celebrated. I remember wondering, *Why hasn't she done anything yet?* I knew she was still mad. My ribs were healed and Canna was still riding hard on the "Brood of hoods" from St. Paul. Had Mom lost her nerve? All I know was that I was feeling defeated.

I behaved as well as I could. Life was easy when

you checked out. I didn't care about anything. I did as I was told or did nothing at all, and it seemed everything was fine. I was now just dumb. I overheard one of the teachers who might get me the following year asking Lanterland about me. Her reply still stings to this day. She described me as "DDS" to this teacher.

The teacher asked her what that meant.

Lanterland then describe me as, "Dumber than dog shit."

I didn't know the plan, or, for that matter, the details, but rest assured, Mom had a plan in place. I knew this, but time was running out. The school year was almost over. She was not getting the breaks she needed. Things just weren't falling into place, and she was grasping at straws. Mom desperately needed Canna to make a mistake, even a small one.

I continued to do as little as I could, since I wasn't going to do anything for those people that didn't like me. I was checked out.

One day I came home with a test that had my regular 'F' on it. This test was what would have passed for a science test in those days. Isn't it strange how when we set up a pattern, we then perform according to that pattern? The pattern is created by doing what is expected of us by our authority figures, according to the information we are receiving from them at the time. This was true in my school assignments because no one was looking at them, since they were always the same, a failure. Science was actually something I liked and was one of the few areas where I did well. This particular test was about biology. A classmate had brought her dog and a litter of pups to school. This was her contribution to our science lesson. The subject interested me, and I listened intently to the student who brought in the puppies. Puppies are a big deal in grade school.

As Mom read the biology test, she got a bit irritated. I said, "Mom, I knew you would not like this test."

She asked, "Why not, son?"

I told her, "Because, I knew the answers."

"What do you mean?" she wondered.

"I could have done this one in my sleep, and do you know why, Mom?"

Mom looked at the red X marks written next to the line of numbers that symbolized the teacher's careless dismissal of my efforts. She read the answers, then looked at me with surprise and said, "You did know the answers, didn't you?"

"You betcha!" I answered.

God, was I proud! I had finally done something Mom approved of. My scribbled writing and unorganized answers were there but were unimportant to Miss Lanterland. Mom recognized that I had the right answers. I had not read the instructions, had not answered in the right spot on the page, and I had not followed the format that was expected.

"This test is an attempt at sex education?" Mom remarked with cold emotion. She was talking to herself.

"Mom, you taught all of us kids this stuff from the very first time I can to remember."

"You betcha," Mom stated, while mimicking me.

She read the questions very carefully. She looked at the multiple choices that were given. The true/false questions weren't any better than the multiple choices. The final straw came with the matching. She looked very intently at the answers I had written in the open spaces, in the margins, on the sides, and along the bottom. The answers were not very legible, but they were there.

Had Miss Lanterland read the scribbling that I had written? The more Mom looked at the test, the bigger the smile on her face became. Part of her amusement was the joy she felt as a mother who realizes that her son was not as bad as she had let herself think, nor as bad as Miss Lanterland had said he was.

The more sinister part was the realization that she had the piece of the puzzle that would get her the upper hand in this game. If she just had enough time, she could get to the right people with the evidence.

If she could be cute, charming, and persuasive, and if her timing was perfect, she just might pull this off. I saw the hope in her desperate eyes. This was the chance that she just might get others to believe, legitimately, that her son was not lazy and dumb.

She saw the chance to prove this in a way that would not be confrontational, and might even be heard above the objections of a power-hungry, dictatorial principal. She hugged me, and with a confident wink that made me think that things might just get better, she said while nodding a yes, "We just might be all right."

She knew intuitively that Lanterland, my teacher, was a 't' crosser and an 'i' dotter. If Mom was right, my teacher's compulsion to be right at all costs would be her downfall. She knew that she had to have irrefutable evidence that her kid was trying and succeeding. She knew that she could teach this child herself and extract revenge at the same time. For the first time in this chain of events, she realized that it didn't require a fight, but that she could resolve the differences with a positive approach for a positive outcome. She had a vision, but could she sell it? For that, she needed more proof.

She had started the planning of this drama. She made a request. Mom asked for my assignments to be written out by Miss Lanterland and sent home. She then asked in writing for Miss Lanterland's assistance in the reviewing and monitoring of all the assignments I had to do. She requested in her best handwriting and in the "King's Own English" that each assignment be detailed in writing so she could follow along. The note was a masterful augment for Mom's involvement in the education of her child. She then stopped writing and put the letter in her best envelope, being very careful to fold the note she had written exactly into thirds. On the envelope, she wrote in her best block printing:

To Miss Lanterland.

As soon as this had been completed, she called Canna, knowing all along that he would not take her call. She left this message with his secretary, "Ask Mr. Canna to please talk with P's teacher, and to ask her to pass along all P's assignments, per my written request. Please, be detailed, as I sometimes get confused, and please, have her do this in writing."

The next day, Canna leaned back in his oak chair and spoke to Miss Lanterland, "I thought I made it clear that every reasonable request was to be honored." He was especially cooperative. "I thought that because I had hurt this boy, you understood that we best be helpful."

He had to be helpful in case he was reported to the school board by Mom. He was sure this was going to happen. The ol' boy, Canna, said, "Miss Lanterland, if I can head off some criticism by being helpful, it couldn't hurt. I'll let her have that concession, this time."

Mom had found a wedge, a tool she could use. This was the first time that Canna had even listened to her request, much less granted the request. She thought that with this success she could move the balance of justice a little further in her son's direction.

Mom prepared lengthy instructions each day, fabricated from the assignments of the day before. This went on for a month. Each letter asked for greater levels of detail, stopping just short of the ridiculous.

Mom was acting in my best interests in her letters to the teacher, yet each letter became more and more demanding. The things she asked for were justifiable, but costly in terms of Lanterland's time and energy.

Miss Lanterland was doing everything she could to comply, until she got fed up and went nuts with frustration. She stormed in Canna's office and yelled at him, "I am not going to be that woman's *nigger* any longer!" The emotional outburst was classic ol' spinster, schoolteacher meltdown. She yelled first, and then shook papers at him. She showed him the "F" I had received, never once stopping to show him the answers written in the margins, written upside down, or written on the back. She just shook the papers at him, until, finally, the weeping and crying started.

Canna gave in and said, "I'll call the bitch and tell her to lay off with the notes and requests."

Mom was waiting for the call. It didn't take as long to come as she thought it would. Canna said to her, "Well, you've had all the attention we can afford to give you and your boy. We are going to have to stop answering your letters. Miss Lanterland is doing all she can to help, and your son is failing anyway. She has other students in that room; your son isn't the only child that needs help."

"Oh, that's interesting," Mom was on her best behavior.

"What's interesting about it?" Canna asked. "We have tried to help, but it doesn't work."

"I thought it was working wonders," Mom said.

"Well, it's not, and I have the papers and tests to

prove it," Canna fired his answer at her.

"I have the same tests that you have, since we copied them at my husband's office on the new Xerox copier. They are complete with the answers written by my son. We have every test, every written worksheet, and everything that was requested, all written down and completed with Miss Lanterland's written instructions. I have corrected them myself."

Mom was on a roll, "I have come to a different conclusion. He is doing just fine. In fact, some of his answers are quite good. Haven't you read the papers?" she queried.

"I'll get back to you," Canna said in an angry tone. Then, he hung up.

Mom smiled at me and said, "I think we are doing okay, so far." She was pleased with herself. Just a few more assignments and she would have all the proof she needed, the proof that her son was completing the assignments and answering the questions correctly. They might not all be perfect answers, but there were enough correct answers to achieve a passing grade.

At this moment, I thought for the first time that things might be all right. I had given up thinking I would be able to go back to the old house on Grotto Street. I guess Mom had diverted my attention to the game of chess she was now playing and had sucked me in, as I was the center of attention. Hope was returning.

Mom had created a sneak learner. I still don't know if the point was to get me involved in the learning process by making me an accomplice to the letters and the intrigue, or if she really wanted me to "Get it" educationally. You know what, it doesn't matter. I learned a lot in those days when we were writing letters. If I could respond to my assignments in a way that was genuine, then Mom was pleased. Pleasing

Mom was more important than pleasing those strangers who hated me.

The motivation didn't matter anymore. I was all right. I was not just all right; I was great, as I watched my mother work hard to accomplish her goals. Add the hard work to the fascination of the game, for real stakes with real outcomes, and you had me interested. I watched Mom that winter and all the way into spring, working hard to create a learning machine (Me). This was her gift. She had created a son, and then she had given him a tool. The tool was not just self-respect, but also a way to organize the world on my own terms. More important was the idea that my way of organizing the world was mine, and there was nothing wrong with that.

I was to learn that life was not always what it seemed, and what seemed to be was often something else. We can do one thing and get results that were not expected, and that's okay. We can take advantage of many things that happen in this world, if we are allowed to act according to our own thoughts. Man, was I having fun. Mom's attention was focused, my attention was focused, and time flew by.

Mom told me after a long, unexpected telephone call form Canna that came shortly before summer vacation, "You flunked the fourth grade." We did not see that one coming. She said, "It's all right; it will all be okay. I will go with you on the last day of school when it will be official."

I now believe that if we'd had a little more time she would have pulled off a small miracle. I believe this, as I know it to be true. This is forty years later, and the truth holds up over time. This was Mom's way of teaching me what was important and what wasn't. She taught, and I learned.

I walked out of Canna's office by myself. I had lost

my temper in Canna's office and was told to leave by my mother. I had yelled at Canna, "You old bastard!" but before I could get any further, Mom sent me packing.

I walked past the secretary's desk and into the hallway in front of the Principal's office, on that last day of school. I noticed the bird's eye, maple floors. I remember the smell of the banana oil used to shine the floors. Every time I smell Banana oil, today, that day rushes into my memory with a shiver.

I walked down the creaking wooden stairs to the main floor. I walked through the big, wooden double doors that led to the outside doors and across the rubber mat between the inside and outside doors. I remember the smells, the weather, and the colors of that old school. I remember every detail of that day forty years ago. I moved my injured soul out onto the concrete stoop in the summer sun, and I stood there.

Mom was still inside fighting with Canna. I could hear her yelling, and I knew she was not going to win this one. Oh, God, did I know the outcome. No one cared that I had learned anything. No one cared that I had overcome a huge problem. Well, Mom did, but no one else cared, especially Canna who was going to get his way.

She had sent me out, because she had sensed my anger welling up. She had sent me outside where I wouldn't do anything I would regret. I wished he would just break my ribs again, so I wouldn't hurt so bad inside, in my head and my heart. I knew that Mom was fighting a losing battle, and so did she.

I wanted to really hurt that "Ol' bastard" for hurting Mom. After all, it hurt Mom more than me. I loved Mom, and I just wanted to tell her. My wishes didn't mean shit. I had caused all this pain for nothing; how worthless can one small boy be?

I stood in the summer sun for what seemed like forever. Mom finally came out, and she hugged me. She was crying, and I was crying. I went home with Mom that day. I knew nothing would ever be the same, and no one would ever know what I knew, nor would I ever let anyone know what I knew.

I was done crying. I swore that I would never let anyone know how bright I was, and yet, it would be the only thing that I would care about for the rest of my life. This was the day that a "Sneak learner" was born; a second birth had taken place. It came from my mother's will and nurturing, and finally, from her pain.

Chapter 4

"Jeffery Canna Lives"

In 1990, I had completed a career in the construction industry. I had done well by the standards of having been born on Grotto Street. I had owned and then sold a profitable construction company. Hence, I had spent the next year fishing, building projects around the house, and for a time, trying my hand as a day trader on the stock exchange.

I was rich at forty and knew that I was not going to risk my good fortune on building a new business. I had done that once, and I had won. That win, along with the help of a tornado taking a piece of property and leaving a big insurance settlement behind, was my ticket to really being rich. The insurance settlement had gone into the stock market, free of encumbrances, and all I had to do was allow it to grow without touching it.

Now, all I needed was a steady income with good health insurance. I needed something to do that wouldn't risk the "Nest egg" I had built.

One day in 1990, I got a call from a friend, Bob, at St. Paul Technical College. Bob got me on the phone and asked, "Why haven't you hired any graduates from my construction program for a while?"

I told Bob, "I'm not hiring anyone, because I have retired from the construction business."

He said, "You'd better stop and see me at school."

A few days later, I did, and he put me in front of his classroom of pipe fitters-to-be and said, "If you guys want to know how to get rich in the construction trades, then this is the guy to talk to." As he left the room, he said to me, "You've got it, teach them something about the construction industry." At the prompting of their questions, I gave them quite an earful, and they listened to me. I was hooked, and so began my teaching career.

I taught for two years at the Technical/Vocational School and was happy. I would never have left if I had not been approached by the University of Minnesota Technical Education Department. They wanted me to teach in the construction trades area.

I had received a Masters in Business Administration in night school. My need for expertise in computer technology had driven me back to school.

I had completed a B.A. in 1973, as a draft dodger during the Viet Nam years. I was able to get a 'C' average, and still work forty hours a week to stay alive. It sounds like a sneaky thing to do, but it was legal and it kept me out of the draft. Finally, in 1973, I drew a high enough draft number to escape the draft, but I had already graduated anyway.

The Masters Degree made me unique in the construction industry. It also made me attractive to the University of Minnesota as an instructor. I loved the University of Minnesota.

The state cut the funding for industrial education in 1995, and my job was history. I had, however, become licensed in High School Industrial Education, so I joined the staff at Northwest Schools.

A year later I was teaching at a middle school, making wooden ducks with sixth graders. What a ball. I was in love with every single one of those darling students, even the "Bad ones" were fun. I heard my name more times than I care to tell anyone. "Mr. P, what do I do next? Mr. P, how do I do this? Mr. P, help me." On and on it went. I was a very happy camper.

As the year was drawing to a close, I was summoned to the principal's office, and the ugly sound of change was present in that conversation, "You are going to school this summer to learn how to run a Synergistic Lab," I heard this lovely woman who had been my principal say. I had taught at the U. of M. for two years where I was exposed to a Synergistic Lab, so I knew what it was.

I replied, "I'm not impressed. Teaching in a room with cubicles that look like early IBM decorating is not my way of hooking kids on the technical arts. Putting them in a cubical and showing them a video is not the way to hook kids on the idea that they could create objects with their will, hands, and most important of all, their hearts. I think this Synergistic Lab will be the death of young souls. It was devised by old men who wanted to organize children into would-be worker bees that would occupy cubicles for the rest of their lives. I'm an old 'Hippie' that believes every soul was placed on this earth to create something."

I continued to argue, "I'll be disappointed, and I beg for part of the program to remain as it is." So, I'd said my piece. I had alienated her with my outspokenness.

But, I wasn't going to change anybody's mind. The Synergistic Corporation already had the school board hot-wired. They had done their job well and I was too late in the game.

I wondered, *What the Hell does a forty-five-year-old rich guy know about how real life works?*

I was not even consulted when the final decision

was made. The die had been cast. With their rush to become the "Synergistic, Cubical School of the Future," I found myself making inquires into a position at one of the district's high schools. It seemed that the district had started to build a new high school. In this new high school was a plan for a high tech computer lab with the latest drafting software.

I thought that new, computer aided drafting software was right up my alley, so I bid on the job. I was a Teachers' Union member with some seniority, although I had not been tenured in the district yet. I needed one more year of experience before I was tenured in this district. This meant that I should stay put for one more year and get my tenure.

I was not worried about the money, I was not worried about loosing my job, and, like the rest of my life, challenge and risk were comfortable on me. I went for the new position and got it. Later, I found out that no one else wanted the job since the learning curve on the software was steep. Also, I didn't know what the other teachers in the district knew, and it was about the principal I was about to go to work for.

The school year ended, the summer came, and then it was soon behind me. We were looking August in the eye. It was time for me to get back to the business of teaching.

On a beautiful, Minnesota summer day, I got up and went to the bagel shop where I enjoyed coffee and a cinnamon raisin bagel. What a day, at seventy-five degrees, sunny, bright, warm, and full of promise. I drove to the old Northwest High School, since it was being used for the staging area for the administration until the new high school was finished.

I needed keys to the new lab because the new high school was near completion. I needed to get into the space and get set up. I wanted to get it all just right for the first day of school.

I parked in the lot of the old Northwest High School and walked up to the front of this school that had been built in the early 1900s. After walking up the concrete steps to an outside landing, I was standing in front of a pair of double wooden doors. I walked into the old Northwest High through the double doors, across the vestibule, through another set of wooden, double doors and up the wooden, creaking stairs to the top. I stopped for a second on the stairs with the most uncomfortable feeling. There was scent of banana oil in the air. The oil must have been used in the past on the old, wood floors. At the top of the stairs was a wooden door with the word 'Principal' in gold block letters with a black border. I opened the door to the office and there was a secretaries' desk in front of a wooden office door with frosted glass. The glass had the name 'Dr. Fritz, Principal' painted in large, block letters.

I thought, *Well, this is just some small anxiety. Get the keys and go to your new room.*

Into the principal's office I went, past the front counter that separated the office into two sections. I went to the secretaries' desk in front of the office and next to the waiting area. The waiting area was lined with straight-backed, wooden chairs that had seated many wayward students while they waited for their turn to get their just deserts. These chairs had also known the worries of many parents that were summoned to the school. Here, in this office, I arrived at Judy's desk, the principal's secretary.

Judy was a good sixty-years-old, and she had been in this office for thirty years. She looked at me and asked, "Can I help you?"

"Yes, I'm Mr. P, the new technology instructor;

can I get a set of keys to my new room?"

Judy put down the folder she was filing and said, "I will tell Dr. Fritz that you're here, and that you need to see him."

"You don't understand; I don't need to see anyone," I insisted. "I just need the keys."

She replied with conviction, "You need to see Dr. Fritz, understand? Now take a seat and wait until I call you." She went into Dr. Fritz's office, came back, and didn't say a word. She didn't even look at me.

I did as I had been told. An hour later, I got up to leave without the keys and started for the door. Judy asked, "Where are you going?"

I told her, "I'm leaving." Now I was mad. Judy looked at me and said, "If you know what's good for you, you'll wait."

I sat down, and a half-hour later the phone rang. Judy answered it and then said to me, "Dr. Fritz will see you now."

This was my new boss. Who in God's name in the education business would not let you have a set of keys, especially when you had been with the district prior to changing schools? This wasn't a job interview; I already worked for the district. I walked into a formal room with a great, big, wooden desk. A man stood up from behind the desk and said, "What do you want? I'm busy building a new school."

I responded with, "I need the keys to the computer lab. I'm Mr. P, the new instructor."

"You will have to come back after you have made an appointment to get the keys. I'm busy building a new school." He shoved his arm out, and, with a jerk, exposed a Rolex watch, looked at it, and said, "Get out of here, and make no mistake about how things are done at Northwest."

I turned to walk out of the office, past the front counter without stopping to make an appointment with Judy, and out into the old Northwest High hallway. I looked at the wooden, birds-eye maple floors and smelled the banana oil. Then I walked down the creaking, wooden stairs, out the double doors, onto the concrete stoop, and into the summer sunshine.

As I stood there asking myself what had just happened, suddenly, it hit me —— "Jeffery Canna lives."

Chapter 5

Dr. Fritz

It had been rumored in the school district that the last thing in this world Dr. Fritz wanted in his school was an almost fifty-something teacher working for him. His preference for teachers was in young, single, non-tenured females, and the more vulnerable they were, the better. He especially liked young, female teachers, who, for whatever reason, had been dismissed by other districts and were desperate for a job.

What he didn't like were teachers who were well established in their area of expertise and backed by the teachers' contract. Teachers who were independent minded and rich, he did not need. In fact, he hated the teachers union and their contract. He hated the rules, and he hated the fact that a contract limited his scope of influence.

"That's a stinking teachers' contract, with all its rules and due process for teachers. Worse yet, the contract favors tenured teachers," I can remember him saying to me.

These teachers would establish their own self-esteem, independent of his approval or disapproval. The game was about control. Dr. Fritz wanted as much as he could get, and he didn't care how he got it.

"This is my school; this is my time. I have earned the right," according to him, "to run my school as I see fit, with whoever I choose to have teaching here."

He had to put up with a small group of "Old hands" that he'd inherited when he had been appointed principal. However, they were dwindling in numbers. Time alone would heal that insult to him, as these "Old hands" would soon retire.

I had not discovered all this in the 1995-96 school year. I had been focused on the technology that I would be teaching. I was laser-focused on that new computer aided drafting lab. It never occurred to me that Dr. Fritz was any different than any other principal. Anyway, I was forty-six, established, and had been happily married to the same woman for twenty-plus years. I had the "Magic bullet" of teaching tenure at the end of the year. I felt I was protected, as the union had made me an officer of the union. Under federal law, no officer of a union could be fired when serving in a union position. A good friend at the middle school had seen to it that when I joined Dr. Fritz's staff, I was made an officer of the union. I did not realize at the time why Dick, the Union President, had done this. I do now.

Dr. Fritz would have to catch me in a felony or find me in a compromised sex scandal to get me fired, and I knew it. I was established in the district with a good track record, so what could Fritz do? When I took the position, I was not concerned with his behavior because I was protected by the contract. Or, so I thought.

Shortly before the kids arrived at school that fall, Dr. Fritz summoned me to his office. I had received one of his infamous "C-Me" notes. The note would be placed in your mailbox and it would say in bold, black sharpie felt pen, "C-Me." Sometimes it would be in red, but always signed in an unreadable scribble or scratch, with his name as bold as could be. The note, as I was to learn in just a few minutes, was a challenge.

I knocked on his door and asked, "Can I please come into your office?" I had very consciously said, "Please." I was aware that our first meeting had not gone well.

My request was met with a stare, a disarming smile, and then an invitation to sit down in the chair which was set at a 45-degree angle to his desk, a great big oak desk.

The only conversation we'd had was in his old office, and, up to this point, conversation had been *terse* at best. The first meeting had been a disaster. Why, now, would he be warm, friendly, and inviting? All I could figure was he wanted something.

He started with small talk, "Tell me about your family?" After I told him a few personal details, he asked me to explain my background. I did, and then he asked, "Why are you teaching?" I explained why I was teaching. All this could have been sincere, but I was not comfortable and he knew it. This seemed to please him.

Then from nowhere came a question that blindsided me, "Do you understand what insubordination is?" I don't even remember how he got to this question, but all of a sudden, I was defending myself. He had a point in mind here, and I was really wishing he would make it and let me go since I was becoming angry. Finally he got to what he was after, "You must understand that insubordination is an offense you can be fired for," Fritz stated this as casually as if he were discussing the weather.

I wondered, *How did we get here? It wasn't even the first day of school yet, and I haven't refused anything he wants.*

"I will document every act of insubordination you commit," again, with the flat tone and the casual attitude. *What does Fritz want?*

"What insubordination?" I asked.

"If I get eight to ten incidents of insubordination, I will fire you," Fritz was goading me.

How did we get from speaking of family and friends to him firing me? I was mad now, hopping mad; I was damned mad. Just as I was about to explode in a burst of anger, I stopped myself and remembered that I had a right to union representation in any situation that a reprimand was involved.

I looked Dr. Fritz in the eye. I calmed myself, took a deep breath, and said, as I would many times in the future, "Dr. Fritz, this conversation is no longer constructive."

I paused again, breathing even more deeply. I took deep, deep breaths while exhaling slowly and counting the seconds that it took to exhale. I had not let him know anything about who I really was or what I really thought. I was being true to my convictions. As I started to get up, he said, in a loud screaming voice, "Sit down! This conversation is over when I say it is, and not one minute sooner! If you don't sit down and shut up, I will write you up for insubordination, right now!"

I wasn't ten years old anymore, and I certainly knew what I could do and what he could do, and this wasn't it. I had worked for some real "Assholes" in my life, but he was the worst I had ever encountered.

I stood up and said in as calm a voice as possible, "I wish union representation."

He yelled at me as loudly as he could, "You'll leave when I tell you!"

I stood up, turned, and walked out. I don't remember what it was he was yelling and screaming at me as I left. I just remember him yelling and screaming.

I walked directly to the union rep's room. Denny,

an "Old hand," looked at me, as I was beet red, and said, "You just left Dr. Fritz's office, didn't you?"

"Yes, I did."

"I could tell where you have been by the look on your face. I can also tell you he wants someone gone. I just didn't think it would be you. He likes to get you mad so you say things you will regret, and if he gets lucky, you will say something stupid that he can use against you in the future. From now on, you don't go into that office without me or the other union rep. Got it?"

"Yes, I got it."

I left the room and walked into the brand new, terrazzo-floored hall of the new Northwest High. I pushed open the fire doors that separate the halls for fire protection. I smelled the new paint and I began to shake. My hands were also shaking and I was mad, frustrated, and ten years old again, with a failing sense of self-esteem and a childhood anger that I thought had been beaten into submission. But there it was; the boy who had failed the fourth grade was right here in this almost fifty-year-old body.

Chapter 6

"The Old Hand Speaks"

The outcome of my visit to the office was predictable, Denny and Sue, the union reps, visited Dr. Fritz and asked for a reprimand in writing. They wanted Dr. Fritz to level a charge in writing, and they knew he wouldn't provide them with any written documentation that might be used to embarrass him. Of course, Dr. Fritz refused. He knew the incident would go nowhere, and anyway, he wanted nothing in writing that might be used against him in court or in front of the school board.

Denny got back to me the following day. He came to my room, sat down alongside my desk, and told me, "Never go into that office again without union representation."

I objected by stating what he already knew. If I had to work in a high school, even a big one, it demanded a certain amount of interaction with the principal that can't be avoided. I told him, "I can't stay below the radar forever."

I tried to think of the situations that I had to interact with the principal, "If a student is a problem beyond the disciplinary reach of the teacher, to mitigate behavior, a meeting with the principal is necessary." This was one example that I used.

A teachers' annual goals meeting is mandated by

the union contract. This is the meeting where the teacher shares with the building principal the objectives to be achieved for the year. This is a holdover from the management-by-objectives fad that took over the business climate twenty years ago. This, like all the fads that have come and gone, leaves a mark on the school system. We get these management procedures in place, and then the system has no way of removing them from the union contract. It was one more example that I mentioned to Denny of mandatory principal/teacher contact.

Denny said, "Don't use the office for anything. If I have a student with a behavior problem, I handle it myself, since we have no support in the principal's office anyway. I have seen Dr. Fritz use students to implicate a teacher in scandals before."

"The need to work with a principal demands some contact," I argued. I admit that I thought I could keep a real low profile and avoid Dr. Fritz as much as possible, yet I knew that there would be a certain amount of interaction that I could not avoid. Goals meetings were an example that I gave Denny. "Get a union rep to go with you," was his solution. "Never be alone with him," was his advice. "Make sure that whoever is with you is on your side," he admonished.

"But we're choosing sides. What's next, bodyguards to accompany me to class?" I wanted to say more, but I didn't say a word. I was making a disaster of the situation, all of which I dismissed as a product of my overactive imagination.

Denny looked at me... a long time silent, "You aren't the first to have trouble with this guy, Fritz. We, the union, have a long history with him. He has an "A" team, and then there are the rest of you. You will learn that if you aren't picked and screened by him, he doesn't want you to work here. In fact, he will work like hell to get rid of you, anyway he can."

Denny went on to tell me, "Dr. Fritz was molded by an administration above him that wanted to hear nothing, see nothing, and mostly, know nothing. They wanted teacher compliance, as this helped to divide staff, pitting each teacher against the other. This teacher unrest was vital to keeping contract wage settlements at a minimum."

"Worse yet," Denny went on, "Dr. Fritz agreed with this strategy and was promoted up on the 'Hill' (The District Center) for his wily ability to carry out the process. He is the poster boy for teacher compliance.

As long as he didn't share his methods with those who could testify in a court, and as long as he gave them, the superintendent and upper management, plausible deniability, then he was a hero. In turn, the administration sold him to the community as the man who makes the busses run on time. Busy people, trained by a mass media and being products, themselves, of a school system that worked the same way for them, are easy to convince that a strict disciplinarian and control freak is the answer to an orderly school."

Denny was allowing his own frustration to bubble to the surface. He stopped himself, regretful of the length his disclosure had gone. He wondered out loud, "I'd better stop before you go to Fritz and share my contempt for him." He was winking at me with that, to determine if I was a loyal union guy he could share secrets with, or someone who would sell him down the river.

I told Denny, "I will come get you or Sue if I get called into the office." He must have decided to trust me; he then told me something I will never forget, "If you are called in to Dr Fritz's office, never be alone. If he calls you out of your room, never be alone with him." Denny's advice was hard to listen to.

I asked, "Why?"

Denny explained, "Dr. Fritz likes to ambush teachers like you."

Now I got scared, "What the hell are you talking about; I'm protected by a teachers' contract, and I'm an officer of the union."

Denny looked at me and warned, "Dr. Fritz will stalk you in the halls, and he will attack the minute you are alone."

"What in the devil are you talking about?" I was certain that I had been imprisoned.

"Well, he likes to catch you off-guard and will try to get you to say things in anger. He will use non-verbal gestures and his body posture to violate your personal space. He will yell and scream at you. He will do anything to get you to loose it. Don't do that; please, don't loose it. Just walk away; please, just walk away." Denny seemed to have been there before.

He went on to explain that if I could just keep my mouth shut around Dr. Fritz, he and the State Union guys could save my job. In his explanation, he went on to say, "You are in for one hell of a battle for the rest of the years you stay at Northwest. Fritz will never give up, and even if you do nothing wrong, he will still try to get you to blow up.

Fritz enjoys his emotional release without the other persons being able to fight back. He loves taunting you, goading you, and getting you to say something he could take out of context and use against you."

Then Denny told me, "If he can't get you to quit, he will eventually make your job so impossible that you will physically get sick. Getting you sick gets rid of you."

"Denny," I asked, "what do you recommend I do? How do I fix this?" I was sincere in my wish for a solution.

"You can leave. You can go back to a middle school or to our sister high school, and you will have given him what he wants. He will not quit until you are dead, or until you leave," this was not the answer I wanted to hear from Denny.

"Why don't we call for a vote of no confidence?" I suggested. A vote of no confidence is a way for a teaching staff to get rid of a principal they don't like.

"We can't," Denny said. "He has a staff of fifty percent non-tenured teachers, and he will keep it that way. Non-tenured teachers don't vote for no confidence, because if they lose the vote, they all get fired. Remember, non-tenured teachers can be fired without cause or any due process. They are employees 'At will'."

"You mean that we have a staff of young teachers in their third year or less." I tried to get this point clear, "Teachers with no rights, or, 'At will employees' that can be fired for any reason without union protection or union rights. They are employed at the pleasure of the school district and serve at the will of the principal. If he decides they are not good teachers, or he just plain doesn't like them, they are released."

"You've got it." Denny went on, "These teachers are so happy to be working that they do what they are told. Then, just as they are about to get tenure, he fires them."

"He can do this?" True shock had taken over.

"Yes, he can," Denny's answer was prophetic.

"Why doesn't the union step in, on the grounds of fairness?" I was serious.

"We can't get a vote at the top of our union to confront this problem. We are a divided staff, and the teachers without tenure have been pitted against those of us who do have tenure. When the few that make it through the tenure window get rights, they are only there because of Dr. Fritz. They are the most loyal to him and become his eyes and ears, telling on other teachers and acting in Fritz's best interest, if they know what's good for them. This divides us even more." Denny had thought about this before.

"Why does this happen; why do we let this happen?" I was really mad.

"It's a matter of economics," he said. "We have so many teachers in this country that the supply is unending. But administrators sell the concept to the public that there is a shortage of teachers. The colleges then lower their entrance requirements, gear up by opening new classes, and *bingo*, we have more and more teachers."

This was Denny's take on the situation, "With a never-ending supply of teachers, willing to work for almost nothing, being supplied by the diploma mills, we keep the system working in favor of the administrators. The system needs to get rid of older, tenured teachers. This keeps the cost of education down and keeps the meat grinder supplied with new, lower paid teachers."

Denny was on a roll. The soapbox was under his feet.

"The next step in their plan will be to bring in adjunct faculty, or part time teachers, as have the State and Jr. College systems. Then, just like in the colleges, they can get rid of benefits, as well. This was done at the college level because there was a shortage of college staff, so part time, unqualified staff was needed to fill the shortage, according to the colleges and universities. I expect to see the same pattern in the high school system as soon as administrators figure out how to do it."

I left a classroom that had been Denny's workplace for twenty years. In the hall, I turned, looked back, and asked myself, *Why am I teaching? What the hell do I need this for?* Then, I remembered the failed child that lives inside my person. That child is with me everyday, an ever-present reminder that I have an obligation to try and help those who might also end up as failed children.

Chapter 7

"Epiphany"

I thanked Denny for his help and left for my room. As I walked back to my classroom, it struck me that the tools I had at my disposal to deal with this "Creep" were tools that didn't even register on Dr. Fritz's radar. He would be looking for an emotional flash point; I could use that fact. He didn't have the ability to think outside the walls of his own insecurities. I was experienced well beyond the limitations of this highly educated, conservative, and Machiavellian administrator. This Fritz seemed to be some kind of throwback to a time and place I didn't recognize.

I, on the other hand, remembered the street fights that I had experienced as a young man while growing up in the construction industry. I knew how to use tools that fell outside the accepted methods of union redress.

As I walked the terrazzo floors of this brand new school, the sterility of the place struck me. I remembered that we had been given instructions to keep the halls free of student work. We were not to hang, tape, staple, or display any student work without Dr. Fritz's permission. If we were given permission, then we were to get a memo on how student work was to be displayed. The location would have to be okayed by the king himself, Dr. Fritz.

The walls were a metaphor for the school's culture. I was still stinging from the incident in his office, so the blank walls exemplified the lack of freedom I was feeling. They represented his lack of trust in the staff who were ultimately responsible for the welfare and education of the children.

I think that this was my moment of epiphany. I think that this was the moment of truth for me. I heard an inner voice; it was as if my mother was talking to me. She had been inspired by harsh events to teach her son how to use a negative incident as a catalyst. Whatever it was she set out to do, it wasn't the outcome she expected. She had taught me to use anger and frustration to motivate me to a constructive end. The lesson also taught me to keep that process to myself. If no one knew what it was that I was doing, they couldn't be critical, and they couldn't hurt me.

I was sure that I was being inspired from someplace deep inside myself. I would like to believe that a higher level of caring could be achieved. What a lesson Mom had taught. She went to her grave believing that she had somehow failed in that horrible year that I flunked the forth grade. Had she lived longer, she might have been counsel to me in this moment of truth. When you think about it, maybe she was? Maybe that inner voice was *hers*. How else was I going to survive this impossible situation? I was on my own, and for the first time, I knew the solution would have to come from within. How to avoid the inevitable, final solution that Dr. Fritz had in mind was an enigma.

I knew that Dr. Fritz would never be watching for a teacher who was operating at a higher level than he had become accustomed to. In his haste to control, he wasn't hiring teachers of integrity. It could be that a professional level of teaching could be injected into this situation.

Maybe Parker Palmer, the teacher's "Guru" and author of "The Courage to Teach" was right, that real teachers have the courage to teach from the heart. This means that as an educator, the student's needs, and the emotions that drive true learning, come first.

This is not rocket science; it is common sense. If you are to teach, then the learner has to feel part of the process. This must be genuine.

It was in this moment that I perceived that it was teaching from my heart that would win the admiration of those I reported to and cared about. I'll tell you who my boss is; it is "The Children," collectively. Yes, it seems goofy, but it's true that after all is said and done, it is the children that I work for. This is the higher calling; this is why I get up in the morning, to answer to my heart.

The symbiotic relationship had been forged by hardship, but there it was. If I taught from the emotional expression of a humanist, then the reaction would be, more often than not, the reciprocal of that equation. Fritz was just an obstacle to get around. If I was real to children, then I neutralized Fritz and was true to my convictions. This worked for me.

As I walked into the classroom, I asked myself what it was that kids needed for them to become adults that were complete and would contribute to our society. Notice that I didn't say, "What the kids wanted." I have given them what they had wanted before, but it didn't work.

Up to now, I had been teaching from a position of "Monkey see, monkey do." I had found teachers who had managed to stay in the classroom for years, and I copied them. This was successful, and I had borrowed many a technique that worked from experienced teachers, but never had I mustered the courage to teach from the part of me that was capable of laughing and crying.

Why then, must I be in a crisis to reach for this tool? I know I will never get an answer to that question. All I know is, I did, and I believe that this was the moment that a "Sneak Teacher" was born.

I knew that it was in winning the respect of students who had never met a teacher willing to genuinely care that I would be able to avoid the treachery of a Dr. Fritz. Dr. Fritz had gotten me by default. I had not been screened by him, and I was not on his "A team," but I could be on the kids' "A team" if I could find a way to teach without getting caught.

Think about this for a second. Why would any parent put his son or daughter in the hands of strangers if it were not for the betterment of the child's welfare? So, it was time that parents got what they paid for and children got what they needed, an education. This was opposed to the babysitting techniques that I had learned from the other teachers.

No more worksheets aimed at keeping large numbers of children busy. No more commercial films intended to entertain them for the ninety minutes that they were with me. No more lectures intended to numb them into semi-sleep, or better yet, sleep. No more military barking at them. I was going to open my mind to customize the learning to each child according to his or her level of knowledge. I was on a roll. I was feeling good about teaching again. I had to remind myself what it was I had come to this teaching profession to do. It was to teach, not baby-sit.

I moved into the classroom, and the first thing I decided was that we were going to hang the student's work up. We were going to celebrate the achievements of children. We were going to celebrate good works, and we were all going to participate in the process of learning. Everyone's work would get hung up.

I also decided that I didn't care where that learning came from. It could come from the students or from me. It didn't matter anymore who the teacher was. All that mattered was that learning was taking place. I walked to the video case where I keep the VHS tapes and took out a copy of Mr. Rogers that I had been using as a source for video clips. I could insert these clips into classroom materials. I had made these videos for the classroom with Mr. Rogers inserted in places that made them quite funny. I put the last one I had made in the machine, and then I took it out and went back to the shelf and got the original Mr. Rogers video that I had taken the clips from. I then turned the lights off and said, "Kids, tell me what this guy does to reach children."

Remember, I'm a drafting teacher. I'm sure that the kids thought that I had lost my marbles. The kids thought I was nuts, because I was out of character for an industrial arts teacher. I didn't care. I just went forward with the questions. Right on through the laughter and the wails of fake pain, I went forward with the discussion. Some of the kids went to sleep, some worked on their computers. But some listened, and some began to ask questions. It was a real dialogue about teaching and learning, and I was learning. It felt good. It was tough, but once again, the threat from a schoolman had brought out the best in me. Adversity was bringing change. I know it was a moment of truth that Dr. Fritz, or anyone for that matter, could not take away from me; it belonged to me.

Chapter 8

"Real Teaching"

I had decided that I was a "Real teacher." I had also decided that a "Real teacher" was different from other teachers, not because he or she cared about students, but because the caring part would dominate. This again sounds as if it were common sense, but it is just not practiced that way in large classroom settings. It can't be practiced that way by most teachers, because it demands a tolerance for chaos. The noise level can become very abrasive to most teachers.

The need for natural groups to form is mandatory for children of a high school level. These student gatherings, with all the group dynamics that make up a social group, are difficult to allow to emerge. The same problem exists in allowing adult groups to emerge; it's noisy and chaotic.

These are all things that drive teachers nuts, because they are judged on how well disciplined the classroom is. It will appear to an outsider as if the teacher has no control, but it is exactly the opposite; the teacher has more control that any administrator could imagine. This control is based on respect, and it isn't perfect, but then, neither is the military approach.

Even in classes of thirty-two and thirty-four

students, where you are asked to baby-sit more than teach, you can find a way to make a difference for as many students as possible. This self-imposed challenge was there to be used as a tool. You might not get to all those who passed through your room, but you could help those who would be helped.

You could allow the students the chance to be working in groups of their choosing, with the operative word being "Working." The group could be trusted to find its own direction, if the basic concept of the classroom was, "Don't be here if you're not going to accomplish some form of learning. I'm here to act as a coach, guide, and resource, but you must put forth the effort." It's not perfect, and it's hard to measure, but it reflects the needs and interests of the students, and not the needs and interests of the teachers, administrators, or any others in the process.

The students who ask questions will get a teacher who pulls a chair up next to them and gives them personalized instruction. The instruction may only be for a moment, but it's delivered with all prejudice put aside.

I listened intently as opposed to talking. I waited for the teachable moment, and then I struck with the answer that captured the imagination. Tests were eliminated, and evaluation was centered on project outcomes and final product quality.

Smiling is a big tool. Calling students by their first names, or, better yet, finding "Pet" names that are humorous to both the student and the teacher really works. Working hard to know the students names is really difficult, since I was seeing ninety to one hundred students every day.

I worked hard at this. Pet names are a way to cement an image and a student to an identity that helped students to be recognized. Continually misprinting words and allowing students to be the teacher and correct me worked wonders to humanize me. Being self-denigrating, and not being afraid to tell a joke at your own expense is a great way to be human. Anything that conveys caring, genuine caring, will aid the process.

Teaching outside your area helps, as well. If students know they can ask any question about anything, then you're the teacher that becomes the resource, the guide. I taught about Judge Roy Bean, a Wild West judge that was uneducated and arbitrary, or I taught them about "Noodling," a way of fishing for catfish with your hands; it didn't matter. Whatever it was that they want to learn in my computer aided, drafting class, it would be taught. We were free to discuss anything. I also made it safe to discuss anything.

I even closed class down for a day to discuss a racial incident. I told the class, "It doesn't matter what subject we need to cover when a black kid is under attack. We need to deal with the immaturity of the students that caused the racial problem. We needed to allow the emotional outflow to pass. We teachers need to lead that discussion to a place where the understanding of the other guy takes place." It wasn't perfect and it wasn't pretty, but it worked. We did that in my classroom, and I'm damned proud of it.

Most teachers at Northwest couldn't, or wouldn't, take the time to deal with this form of teaching. The difficulty was that "This is not my job" was a common statement among teachers. "I teach English," or "I teach biology, and it's not my job. I don't have to deal with problems that are difficult."

In fact, in our school, if Dr. Fritz had caught me talking about racial problems, he would have written me up and reprimanded me for interference with the counselor's responsibilities. Well, I made it my responsibility, and honest discussions were held in my room. I was a "Sneak Teacher" and damned proud of that, too.

There's no question about it; if I had gotten caught, I would have at least been reprimanded, or at the worst, fired. I always said to my class, "You didn't hear this from me." I went where students needed to be in the lessons, not where the teacher needed to be. I got really good at avoiding the reprimand. I was able to teach what needed teaching, and guess what? The level of sophistication in the drawings of the students, the subject I was responsible for, went right through the ceiling. We were *cooking*, we were working harder than I had ever seen students work, yet the students would say to each other, "Take P's class; he's easy."

Learning is not hard; teaching is hard. Learning is fun and it doesn't hurt. Teaching hurts, but not because it demands long hours and deep research, but because it demands that the teacher grows and learns along with the students, and it demands that the teacher digs deep into the emotional abyss and finds the courage to teach from the heart and then the head. It demands that you face your own demons and learn to conquer them. It's not easy to keep growing at fifty, but it can be done.

A routine of learning will emerge, and the kids will seek the consistency that this routine brings, but it changes each quarter with each new group of kids. What worked with one group might not work with another. This style of teaching demands that you be willing to change, and that you make change a constant in the tool chest that you've developed.

I was absolutely amazed at what the students would do for me. The drawings and knowledge of mechanical and architectural engineering and the computer program were on the level I had only seen in industry.

In the six years that I taught from the heart, I had the privilege of seeing one student go to work in an electrical contracting house as a draftsman, right out of the high school classroom. I also had a young man go to work for a fire safety design group. This student was so good at computer-aided drafting that they took him under their wing and educated him as an engineer at the University of Minnesota, free of charge to the student.

I was *cooking*. The summers flew by and the falls were great. It gave me the chance to meet new talent. To me, these weren't just kids anymore, and they weren't just my charges anymore; they were talent waiting to be discovered.

To encourage students, all you had to do was listen to them. They would tell you what it was they were good at. I talked less and less in class and listened more and more. If I caught a student displaying a talent, any talent, I was on to you, and you didn't stand a chance. You were hounded and encouraged until you developed that talent. I didn't care what talent it was, either. It could be anything you wanted, like a skill you wanted to improve or something you wanted to learn. Worse yet, your classmates would join in and the group would not allow you to sabotage yourself. Group sanity demands the best you have to give.

The kids were the ones who understood, intuitively, that they had a good thing going. They would say to their friends and to their younger brothers and sisters, "Take P's class; it doesn't matter if you like drawing or not. He's great; it's my favorite class."

Students talked among themselves, and what they said to each other was this, "Don't ever talk to administrators about what happens in P's class. All you have to say when administrators ask is that P's your favorite teacher and he's great, and then, just shut up. If they ask why, just say you don't know."

Students had figured out that it was not in their best interest to share with administrators the day-to-day workings of the class. I didn't teach this; I didn't encourage this; I didn't even discourage this. I was always benign, at best, when this was the subject of discussion.

Kids are not blind or stupid. They figured it out, and the smart ones made up the strategy that would protect their interests. It also became the norm after a while. I don't mean to tell you that everything was perfect, because it wasn't, but it was good.

It was easy to give good marks, as I was customizing the curriculum for students according to their talents. This was a lot of work for me, and it was work I couldn't get caught at.

Let me tell you, though, when a parent gets a teacher that their kid talks about, it is unusual. When their kid also gets a good grade on top of all that, it gives a sense of pride and of forward progress that nothing else in the world can compare to. To have kids liking school is not that unusual, but to have kids raving about a class gives the teacher leverage.

I knew it couldn't last, not with Dr. Fritz at the helm, but I was determined to go as far as I could, and for as long as I could. I knew that I would be failed just like that kid who stood on the steps of Lincoln Elementary School so many years ago. Those who stood to gain the most from what I was doing wouldn't even take the time to hear me out. Dr. Fritz and his co-conspirators would simply fire me. For that matter, they wouldn't even try to understand what it was that

I was doing. The things that I did in the classroom were outside their level of understanding. It still is to this day. Well, all of this was all right. I would, however, have to remind myself that at the very least, I'd had my moment in the sun. The worst part of teaching this way and the best part of teaching this way is that it is not widely known to the general public that this level of accomplishment is possible. It is hidden from the spotlight, but, so what?

Chapter 9

ZJ

ZJ came to us from our sister school. ZJ had gained a reputation for "Rippin' off" other drug users and had burned a lot of bridges at the other school.

He was a user himself, but his parents didn't, or wouldn't, believe in his addiction.

His favorite trick was to set up a drug deal in school and collect in advance for the drugs. You can guess the rest; he never shows up to deliver the drugs.

That is how he got his handle, ZJ, short for "Zero Junk." He had not resisted when the name was given to him by his fellow junkies in school. Like any label that was associated with drugs, he wore it like a brand name on a soup can. The plan was to use every marketing technique his pusher and handler had developed through years of experience with high school junkies to keep ZJ hooked and productive as a drug "Rep." At the age of fifteen, selling drugs was his profession.

Just like any large pharmaceutical enterprise, the management was very active in keeping the drug reps productive. The difference was that in this game, the reps were young junkies hooked on the products they were selling. This made both the supplier and the salesman far more demanding of each other. The handlers had the upper hand and they knew it, since they had the medicine that the junkie needed to stay well. This is how it was with ZJ when he arrived from our sister school.

ZJ's mom was in total denial of the fact that her son was immersed in the drug trade. She was sure that whatever her son was into, it was just a youthful indiscretion. She loved the boy, maybe a bit too much.

Her older son had been the same way, and outside of a few small problems with the law, she rationalized that ZJ was fine, just as his older brother had been.

According to ZJ's mom, the school had labeled ZJ as "Learning Disabled" and this had led to all his problems. She blamed the fights and acting out in class on the labeling that went along with a special education designation. She would also argue that bullying must have been taking place. Because of these and other reasons, ZJ's mom had requested a transfer to Northwest. ZJ was all for this as he had exhausted the market at the other school and needed new "Suckers" to run his scam.

The other school had become a dangerous place for ZJ and his sidekick, Low Down. The kids all knew his game, and several older users had threatened his life. This was no small threat to ZJ. He knew that there were users that would really hurt him if they got the opportunity. He had ripped off as many users as he could without getting killed. He knew that he would have to get Low Down to go with him to Northwest, because LD, as he was known, would watch his back. LD was the half of the team with the brains, and ZJ knew it. The administration at our sister school went along with both transfers, since it solved two of their biggest problems. Now, they didn't have to worry about these two getting killed on campus. This had been a real threat to the administration, and they'd treated it as a real possibility.

ZJ was a drug user, and he was pushing dope to feed his habit. It was a fact that we, as teachers, all knew he was a pusher; the staff lunch hour was often a speculation session as to his use and selling methods. We were sure as to ZJ's mission and methods, yet ZJ's Mom was so conned by ZJ that she had pushed and advocated ZJ's agenda to be moved to Northwest High.

By the time ZJ first appeared in my classroom, I had already acted on my epiphany. I had all but thrown the established drafting lesson plans out the window, and we had started talking about design and the relationship of design to social needs.

I was also listening closely to how high school students related to each other. I was gaining a reputation for being a teacher who, regardless of your interests, was someone who's class you would want to take because it was fun and interesting.

Well, I also attracted the losers, and I didn't discourage them from coming to my class because I believed that I could help all of them. ZJ and his buddy, Low Down, known as LD, showed up for my class just as fall turned into winter.

ZJ and LD's reputations arrived in my room long before they did. The good kids with a real desire to be part of whatever it was that took place in my room had warned me about those two. But I had no idea of the trouble they would bring to my life. Isn't it strange that the kids have a better understanding of the facts in a school than the adults who are charged with their well-being?

From a students' point of view, the story went like this; ZJ would make a drug deal in school and then set up an off-campus delivery spot. ZJ would never "Carry" on campus, because the drug dogs that visited unannounced would someday reveal the drugs. He was also aware that possession of drugs in school would get him expelled. This was a fate worse than death since school was the market place for his trade. If you were stupid enough to pay him in school, you would get a bogus pickup point and he would keep your money. It didn't take long for the word to spread throughout the student population that this was the way things would be.

ZJ, himself, had taken pride in the name that had been given to him. He was proud of his ability to con and to charm. The name was a symbol of his status in the drug community.

His partner, LD, had imitated ZJ in every way and worshiped him as he had all his life, what little life he'd experienced by age fifteen. He would do whatever ZJ asked, because they were tight. LD imitated him in every way, in his dress, music, speech, gestures, and even the gait that ZJ walked was copied by LD. Even his name, Low Down, came from ZJ. ZJ had given it to him back in middle school, when LD would use his powers of persuasion to get the low-down, slang for information.

It would only be fair to tell you that neither one of these two came from the ghetto. Quite the contrary, they both came from wanna-be "Yuppie" families that drove SUVs and lived in big houses. This wasn't about uncaring parents or a lack of social status.

It wasn't about children with weight problems or physical features that didn't measure up. It was about having fun. Both boys were very attractive physically, well-fed, and came from stable, middle-class homes. There were certainly times when their families had struggled, but for the most part, these were solidly middle-class kids. Don't kid yourself; they didn't deal because they needed the money. Instead, both these boys loved the drugs, the status, the fun, and especially the *Sex*.

The parties were legendary at our sister school. Every time I had heard about such parties, I thought they had been exaggerated to enhance the dramatic effect. The stories were part of the sell that ZJ and LD had spread to market drugs. In fact, the boys' handlers scripted the stories for them. They were quite effective at creating gossip. It was the best "Come On" that the dealers had, especially the sex tales; they were always a big hit with the other boys. High school age boys love to hear girls-gone-wild stories, even if they aren't true.

The dealers had created a myth which put drugs and drug users into the cool group. You were really cool if you used drugs *and* lived the life of a pusher.

I had no way of proving it, but I'm sure that there were gang influences in the mix, with ZJ and LD being the street salesmen for some really bad characters. It seemed to me that their dealing methods were much too sophisticated to have been conceived of by two junkies looking for a good time. The two were a real hit sensation in the halls of Northwest High.

Chapter 10

First Day

My first few days in class with ZJ and LD were uneventful, since they both slept in class. On most days, they were both high from the night before. This is not uncommon behavior for high school junkies. I had seen it many times before. In fact, it is very easy to ignore these guys, because as a teacher with thirty-two kids in the room, you're so happy that these guys aren't raising hell that you just let them go ahead and sleep. When they are not hung over, most high school junkies are a handful. When they are sober, most high school junkies are so hyperactive that they can't sit still. To get them to concentrate for more than ten seconds is a real feat.

One day during the second week of class, as LD and ZJ became conscious, they didn't quite know how to take me. As all high school ninth graders would think, the easy way to find out what a teacher will do is to test the teacher's emotional limits.

The first test that these two came up with was to see how far they could go before they became a problem? At first, they just talked in class. I really didn't care, since I had already gone through the tough, first week of instruction where I taught the basic moves of the software program.

The basics were well under way, and I was only

instructing for about ten minutes a day, now. Just one new skill a day, just enough to build an inventory of skills in the computer program, one move at a time. One drawing concept married to a computer move. The drawing concept was hidden under the computer move so that learning seemed easy to students.

If I taught how to modify a line, then line weight was a given as the drawing concept. The two could not be separated from each other as I taught the line modification. This teaching method is one way that a teacher who has thought through the process of learning can use guile to get kids to learn difficult concepts and processes. The students, without really thinking that they were taught anything, have learned a simple computer move and an intellectual concept. The two ideas are married to each other in such a way that they are invisible to the student.

The unintended consequence of this way of teaching is that students will tell other kids about the class being so easy, and that anyone could do it.

What they don't understand is that it didn't happen by accident. The process was well thought through and delivered in a way that appealed to all learning styles. In addition, it was active, hands-on learning, where the head and the hands were engaged in such away as to access more than one area of the brain. Let me point out a slogan from the University of Wisconsin at River Falls, "Hands on, Hearts on, Heads on."

It is a way of learning that takes the teacher out of the equation, once the concept is taught, and allows the student to seamlessly gain confidence and knowledge at the same time. It is a lot of work, but if it is done properly, the payoff is exceptional.

To ZJ and LD, the set-up to this learning style had been lost in a drug-induced sleep during their first week of school. Of course, they were behind even before we got started.

This is so typical of students that are driven by their addictive diseases. They end up missing the instructions that are the pivotal points of the rest of the learning. They miss all that is taking place around them. They are lost in a sequence of events that they couldn't understand if they tried, since they have missed the basics that are necessary to building skills. The pattern keeps repeating itself, until they are so far behind their peers that they give up and act out their frustrations in the classroom.

ZJ and LD hadn't even been there for the, "How to start the drawing" lesson, so the two were totally lost, and frankly, they didn't seem to care. Their agenda was clear to them. It had nothing to do with learning or how to draw. It was, however, going to be an education for me.

They learned that their talking didn't bother me, especially if they keep it to themselves. They started asking each other how to escalate the testing. What was next?

It didn't take long. The next test was subtle and took a couple of days to set up. They were experts at it. Each of them knew the other's moves before he made them. It was a scripted dialogue with ZJ in control at all times.

Every chance they got, they would kid around about "420." If I were within earshot or directly involved in the conversation, they would make a reference to 420. The conversation was aimed at getting some kind of response from me.

Hitler's birthday was on April 20, or, 4/20. This had meaning to a specific group, the Goths in our school, who were known for their marijuana use.

The Goths were kids that used black finger nail polish and liked to wear dark clothing. These kid's values were on display as they wore their rebellion on their backs. ZJ wanted to know these people for obvious reasons; they were potential customers.

The other group that would respond to the 4/20 jokes were the junkies and casual drug users, since the time, 4:20 P.M., was when the kids were home alone, waiting for parents to return from work. It was party time.

4/20 was also the day that Columbine High School met with tragedy in what ZJ and LD described as the coolest act of rebellion known to man and history.

What was also being tested was my reaction to the joking. If I ignored it, as I did, then I could be a drug user or sympathetic to the user. I was neither, but the possibility existed, according to ZJ's handlers. It might be that I just didn't care, just like a lot of teachers who have learned to pick their battles. I *had* learned to pick my battles, and this was one I couldn't get support for in the front office. What the two boys didn't know yet, but would find out, was that there was no support for me in the front office, at all.

As their plot became clear, I made a statement to the class that I was a "Tea Totaler" and hadn't touched a drop of alcohol in twenty-eight years.

ZJ immediately chimed in, "Yeah, dude, but you get real mellow on *'The Weed'*."

I replied that I didn't use any drugs.

The retort was instantaneous from ZJ, "Right, you were a Hippy, right? You're old enough to be a Hippy. My dad was a Hippy and he smoked every day. You must have been a Hippy or you were in 'Nam. Either way, you smoked; all you guys did back in those days, and most of you still do."

Dead silence filled the room, as all attention was

now focused on my response. I remember thinking, *How do I establish creditability now?* I had tried "The Weed" once. I had hated it and had never tried it again. If I was to be honest with them it might be viewed as a line of crap made up by me to please the administration, or it might just be viewed as disingenuous.

Finally, I got my bearings and I decided to just tell the truth. It's funny, but with kids, the truth always works. It is recognized as the truth by kids, and you become a trusted leader when you speak honestly about life's experiences.

Finally, after what seemed an eternity, I said, "Ya know, I did try grass once. I didn't like what it did to me; it made me sleepy and disoriented. I hated the feeling of disorientation, so I've never tried it again." I was baring my soul, hoping that it would not encouraged anyone to experiment.

There it was, out on the table, just exactly as it had happened. What now?

LD came back with, "Right, and next you will be telling us you didn't inhale, and that you didn't have sex with that woman."

Once again, ZJ had control of the audience, and he and LD knew it. They were both convinced that I was an old Hippy with a lifetime "Weed" habit. They were convinced that I had just been playing the schoolteacher part. They thrived on hypocrisy. If they could brand me as a Hippy, then they had accomplished a good day's work. They knew that I was popular with the same students that they considered their clients, and they were well on their way to being able to take what was said in the classroom out of context. The ability to paint me as a user was important, and they had a good start. According to the ZJ and LD marketing plan, all "Cool teachers" were drug users.

Once again, the rules of manipulation were working against my goals. I felt the same hopeless feeling that had haunted me throughout the opening round with the two young junkies. Please believe me, I still thought that I could win them over and improve their lives, even if just a little. My grandest hope was that they would turn to me for help if they hit bottom.

Chapter 11

A Tale of Two Students

The next step for ZJ and LD was to try and establish leadership of the classroom. The best way to accomplish that was to disrupt the flow of work in such a way as to not get thrown out of class, yet still disrupt it enough to take over. This was a strategy that had been discussed and scripted by "Big Guy," ZJ and LD's handler. After the two of them had reported back on all their classes, a plan was laid out for every class with the objective of maximizing drug sales. My class got a special look because I had attracted an audience of kids that fit the "User" profile.

My room was full of potential users. This class was loaded with mainstreamed, Special Ed. kids. I was going to get extra attention from the dealers, as my classroom was a great niche market within the larger marketplace.

Special Ed. children are high-risk candidates for drug use. The more frustrated that they become with a system not designed for their learning styles, the more they begin to believe they are second-class citizens.

Just think about it for a second, we label them as Learning Disabled (LD), Emotionally Behaviorally Disturbed (EBD), and Title One Reading Deficient. We talk about them behind closed doors, seal their school records, and have special conferences with their parents.

What more could we do to isolate this population and label them. Guess what they turn to? Drugs and alcohol are a way of escaping the pain and disgrace of being different. Special Ed. kids are statistically over-represented in the larger category of the addicted.

Big Guy knew this; Drugs Inc. knew it, too. LD and ZJ were taught this by Big Guy who knew it from his training as a drug counselor.

ZJ and LD's objective was to marginalize my position as leader, or if I would allow it, to simply take over.

Sometimes, older teachers who are waiting for their retirement day to come will simply stand back and allow the students to run the class. As long as it doesn't go to the front office, this was the easy way out. I was an older teacher, so this angle had to be tested.

The two boys came into the room wide-awake and ready for business. This should have been a clue; they were not high today as they had been every day up to that point. In hindsight, it was just that I didn't get it. I was thinking like a teacher at this point. I was thinking that this was just what two ninth graders do when they are doing what ninth graders do. I thought they tested the teachers for a weakness and then exploited it for their own purposes. What I didn't understand was that I was up against an effort organized by adults that had been honed by trial and error many times before. Who said Darwin was dead?

The attack began as soon as I tried to take attendance. The names of students were mimicked, then ZJ and LD were saying "Here" right at the moment when the students would respond to their names. They echoed students that called out "Here" by saying "Here" at the same time as the student did, making it impossible for me to hear or take attendance.

This was most disheartening, yet not enough for me to send them out of the room. The two were very careful to avoid being caught, by accusing other students and then laughing when I was wrong.

I called for quiet in the room but it didn't work. The two continued to bully me into allowing them to do what they wanted. They thought that I would just give up and allow them the leadership position. Well, I didn't. I went over, stood next to them, and asked them to leave the room.

"Just stand in the hall until I tell you otherwise," I said, as I directed them to the hall.

It took a repeated effort, but as they sensed that I was about to call the office for help, they finally condescended to my request and retreated to the hallway.

After a while, I finally let them back into the class, but I knew from that point on I was in for a rough time with these two. If I had only known how rough, I would have been even more assertive.

The next day the same thing happened at role call, yet there was something different. The two stopped short of getting invited to the hall. I sensed a new resolve in these two. The other thing that I had not counted on was the teamwork and the sophistication of the two. Their timing had become improved, and I was certain that they had been practicing the routine.

I remember thinking to myself, *What the hell is going on here?*

Understand, also, that I knew I was not going to get a lot of help from the office. So I developed a discipline philosophy that was mine, and not dependent on the office. The office was only a last resort, not a part of my day-to-day working routine. I also knew that Dr. Fritz would use any effort at discipline that involved the administration as a weapon. He would turn the situation around and twist it to make my life miserable.

As a teacher in this school system, I knew that the office was not a place to look for help or support. Any trip to the office by a student was an opportunity for the administration to grill the students on what I had done wrong in the situation. It gave the administration ammunition with which to degrade me. All the teachers in this school district have learned that if you are an older teacher, you will be open to attack by the administration if you send a student to the office. The object here is to make your life so miserable that you never send anyone to the office, unless it's a life or death situation.

I was already in trouble with the administration, so I was bound and determined to keep this problem in my classroom.

The office didn't care about "Drugies" in the classroom anyway, as long as they didn't have to deal with them. Some of them were even of some value to the administration as snitches and spies. Using children as a management tool is a perfectly acceptable way to achieve teacher compliance. It doesn't matter that it is unethical or immoral. It works, and that's all that matters.

ZJ and LD used this tactic for several days with the outcome not changing a bit. The mimicking would start, and I would send them to the hall. As insane as this might seem, the limits were tested every day in the same way. The same behavior, day after day, and each time the two of them were expecting a different outcome, yet were getting no change.

I was damned consistent in my behavior modification attempts. I wanted a change in behavior, so the same thing happened every day, without fail. Maybe we were all expecting a change. I don't know why I would expect things to change. I was doing things, without alteration, that had worked in other situations.

I was not adapting to the new tactics the two were using. It finally occurred to me that I was going to have to come at this thing from another angle. Besides, the rest of the hour had started to become a test of wills with these two. They were expanding their efforts to test me for the whole hour. Their behavior became nagging and not particularly inventive.

Finally, they started to escalate their disruptive behavior, almost as if it had become personal for them. They were developing a real hatred for me, and I did nothing to conceal my dislike for their behavior. I had not personalized it yet, and I swore to myself that I would not let it come to that.

What made this worse was the fact that this class wasn't the best class I'd ever had. It was loaded with Special Ed. students that had been mainstreamed. I had made my room a welcoming place for Special Ed. students, which meant that I was willing to put up with a lot of acting out and disruptive behavior. This was different. The Special Ed. kids had a pair of peer leaders, LD and ZJ, who were working hard for their hearts and minds. I was still a teacher with all the baggage that goes along with being a teacher. I wasn't a peer, as LD and ZJ were. I was losing the battle.

Their disruption made it hard on the Special Ed. kids, because I had to be very structured in the room to deal with ZJ and LD. Structure was something that made Special Ed. kids go nuts. What made it harder yet was that Special Ed. kids are the first to get on board with a disruptive student, since they are very needy and impulsive to begin with.

Special Ed. students have been tortured by endless hours of seat time by the time they reach high school. Death by lecture is how they describe it. These students tend to be hands-on learners without a lick of patience for an academic lecture. They want to be on their feet; they want to be doing, not sitting. This is gender neutral, because both girls and boys in this learning style are active, hands-on learners.

By this time in high school, they have also begun to develop compensating skills to cope with the sit and learn style that most of them have been subjected to for all the years they have been going to school. The compensating skills have little to do with the written word or the lecture format of learning. They have found other ways of learning that teachers don't recognize as legitimate.

What made these Special Ed. children even more interesting to ZJ and LD, was the fact that no matter how well I had designed my course to meet their needs, by this stage in their school careers, these Special Ed. children had been so damaged by misunderstanding and a factory-school model, that their instinct, anger, and impulsive behavior would come to the surface under pressure, every time.

They were easy prey for ZJ and LD. They were also "Crowd" building blocks for attaining critical mass in a classroom to achieve their ends. Once LD and ZJ could show the rest of the students that they had a following, they could use group psychology to get the class to see things their way.

As the intensity in my room built and the disruptive behavior grew, I could feel the leadership of the classroom passing to a sixteen-year-old junkie and his lieutenant. I was now beginning to panic, and I'm sure this is exactly what ZJ wanted.

I could not give into it or my days as a teacher

were numbered. I may be in a classroom but little, if any, teaching would take place. I didn't come this far to be outdone by a kid, or what I thought was a kid. ZJ and LD were gaining control and I was frightened.

I needed ZJ to make a mistake of some kind. I needed to end the power contest long enough to re-establish the control of the classroom and reshuffle the order of authority. If I could get ZJ to screw-up enough to get him kicked out for a couple of days, I had a chance to win the hearts of this group of kids back. I had to reestablish myself as the role model.

In an intuitive moment, it came to me. A conversation that one of the kids had with me a day or two before had revealed the fact that ZJ's older brother had been charged in a drug deal gone bad. It was just a snippet of information, but I hoped it would be enough to get him to overreact. I needed an outburst that would send him away for a day or two.

The information that I had received was not complete, or for that matter, it may not even have been truthful, but still, there was a chance I could use it.

In a flash, I made eye contact with ZJ. It was the first time on that day I had looked into his eyes. He was higher than a kite. *Oh, my God,* I thought, *his pupils are as big as saucepans, and his hands are shaking.* There was no question about it; he was high.

I thought that maybe I could turn him over to the office for being high; my mind was going a million miles an hour, now. No, no, that one won't work; the office doesn't give a damn if he's high. I had not seen him take drugs, and I was sure he was not packing drugs on him. Those were the only two conditions that would get him into trouble. I didn't have the evidence, but... could I lie? I didn't want to use the information I had been given earlier in the day, but it was starting to look like the only tool in the box, even though it meant confrontation. Seconds passed, and my mind was made up.

In the second that it took to make eye contact, a PhD's worth of mental activity had taken place. It's amazing how you have to make split-second decisions in the classroom and then live with the consequences. Now I was going to have to operate on my wits. In a few seconds, I would not be able to take it back. If I act, then I must be willing to live with the consequences. In a nanosecond, I weighed the benefits without much thought for the consequences, and then I decided.

I said it right into ZJ's face, "How's Zeke?"

ZJ now narrowed his eyes and his face went tight. I had him. His body gave him away, and the gamble had worked. Now, all I had to do was work it. As cool a character as ZJ thought he was, he was still a kid, and worse yet, he was high and not in total control of his emotions or thoughts.

"What the hell do you know about Zeke?" ZJ's question was telling.

"I know the police are looking for him," this was a gamble on my part; I really didn't know if the police were looking for him.

"Fuck You!" ZJ flipped me the bird as he said it.

I had him, swearing in class got you a day of suspension. In fact, in front of thirty-two students, it wouldn't be tolerated by the administration. They had no choice but to act. Ironic, isn't it, that being high in class is okay, but just say, "Fuck," and out you go.

Later, I learned that the drug deal his brother had been involved in was a drug deal gone bad. His brother, having delivered the drugs, had not been paid so he ran over the buyer. Nice role model for his younger brother, eh.

I walked to the phone, called for a hall monitor, and asked for assistance getting ZJ to the office.

ZJ was no longer at his seat; he was walking toward me in a very deliberate manner. *What the hell is this?* I wondered, *Is he going to hit me?* His fists were clenched in anger. He looked into my eyes and I could see the anger, years and years of anger all gathered into a fifteen year old package. How do we produce a kid this angry in just fifteen years?

LD was now on his feet and racing towards ZJ. Just as ZJ came at me and was winding up, LD grabbed his arm at the apogee of his swing and pulled ZJ off balance. The two stumbled backwards and the blow was never forwarded.

"Think, ZJ; if you hit a teacher you're going down for the count!" LD was shouting.

The two swung around to face each other. "I don't give a fuck!" ZJ stated with total abandon.

"Come on, ZJ, think," LD was ordering him now.

Those thirty seconds seemed like an eternity, and it seemed like it took forever to get ZJ under control, but LD did a good job. It was obvious that it wasn't the first time he had done it. Under other circumstances, it would have been a heroic deed, but given what had just happened, I doubted I would be thanking him.

The room was a mess. Desks had been scattered everywhere, since ZJ had put on a pretty good show by throwing desks every which way when he had approached me. The kids were scared, I was not happy, and I was a bit afraid that the office would turn this one around and used it against me.

In walked our hall monitor, a small woman of sixty with thinning blonde hair and a slight frame, and she was not about to be trifled with. Grace asked me, "What do you want me to do?"

"Just take ZJ down to the office," I was demanding at this point.

"What happened here?" Grace was looking around the disheveled room.

"Grace, just take him out of here, but be careful because he's high," I was warning her.

"He tried to hit you?" Grace inquired?

"Ask the class; they saw it better than I did?" I looked for some support in the room.

"What happened here?" Grace asked, as she looked to the class.

I gave them a reassuring look and said, "Go ahead and tell her."

One of my more loyal students, a young hockey player named Hank, said, "He tried to hit the teacher."

I couldn't have asked for a better response if I had planned it. ZJ, needing to keep his reputation intact, looked Hank in the eye and yelled, "Fuck you!" The tone was threatening. It was intended to keep a fellow student intimidated. Hank wasn't buying the threat and ZJ knew it. I thought I saw a flash of surprise on ZJ's face.

Grace had been present for the second "Fuck you!" I was off the hook, as she wouldn't tolerate the swearing. She had support in the office as the hall monitor. Administration had no choice. With Grace, they had to support her efforts or lose control. I really hoped that I had effectively transferred the disciplinary function to her and off my back.

Off went ZJ and LD to the office, but on her way out of the door, Grace looked at me with a weird look and left with both of them.

I was hoping that LD would get painted with the same brush as ZJ. Even if I hadn't gotten rid of them both, I had gotten rid of ZJ for a couple of days. This would help.

Chapter 12

The Set Up

ZJ and LD ended up at the office of Nancy, our Vice Principal, after being escorted out of my room by Grace, the hall monitor. The number of times these two boys had made this walk to the office is uncountable. It always occurs to me that the techniques we use to discipline young junkies are always the same and always ineffective. We do, however, perpetuate this dog and pony show.

Nancy was an ambitious Vice-Principal. She had been in Dr. Fritz's dominion for about six years now. She would do exactly what Dr. Fritz told her to do, always. The slender, dark-haired athletic woman had graduated from this very same high school. Impeccably dressed in the suit of a businesswoman, this woman was all business. She knew that the shortest distance between her job and a principal's title was through Dr. Fritz's influence. No question about it, she was ambitious, and had a clear vision as to how she was going to get what she wanted.

ZJ and LD were told to take a seat in Nancy's office, but not before she had talked to Grace. She got the gist of what had happened but still needed details. She leaned back in her chair, took a deep breath, and stared at ZJ. She didn't say a word, just stared. ZJ was higher than a kite. Could she sense this?

Finally, she asked, "Well, what happened ZJ?" Nancy was almost pleading and playful at the same time. She was good at this.

ZJ was high, and he knew that he would be in trouble with Big Guy if he blew it in Nancy's office. LD was there to help him out as he had helped in the classroom, but he'd better block out the zoo going on in his head. The drugs were really kicking in. The drugs were taking him places that had nothing to do with the business at hand. LD was thinking this was routine, so the drug high was a nice distraction.

Nancy was looking for something besides the truth to come out of this conversation. ZJ didn't know that yet. Nancy was worried that as high as he was, he might not understand what she was about to tell him, that she needed his cooperation. She knew it was a great opportunity to please Fritz. All situations were an opportunity to please the boss, but this was especially sweet, as it was Fritz's wish to target 'P' for dismissal. He had made that perfectly clear to Nancy and his other cohorts. If you wanted to advance here, or anywhere else in the district, you helped Dr. Fritz get what he wanted.

Nancy knew very well that she could send ZJ back to their sister school where it was reported his life may be in jeopardy. She held a lot of power over ZJ's destiny. Now, high as he was, she was going to make a deal with him. She just knew she could get what she wanted.

"Shut the door, LD," Nancy commanded.

LD, not in quite as much trouble as ZJ, smirked and said, "Shut it yourself." LD was testing how much would she take and how much trouble they were in.

Testing her was not the right thing to do at the moment. Nancy wasn't about to take any lip at this point. She stood up from her desk, looked LD right in the eye, and snarled, "Look, you little junkie, I can have a piss test done in seconds if you sass me again, and that will get you suspended."

This was something that Big Guy wasn't going to like, and that meant the end of cheap drugs and cheaper sex for LD. What Nancy didn't know was, it really didn't matter what she said or did. Big Guy was the boss and all that was happening here was compliance. LD knew he had to go along and get along with her to avoid trouble with Big Guy. Nancy didn't care why she was getting compliance; she was getting it, and that was all that mattered.

Nancy sat down as soon as LD closed the door, and the bargaining began.

"You guys want to tell me what happened up in P's room?"

ZJ then recounted the tale, but he failed to mention the part about making threats to the teacher's person. He wanted her to believe that I was at fault, and that any rational human being would have reacted in the same way. Nancy knew these two from other, past encounters. She knew that they were leaving important details out, and normally, she might even have pushed them on it, but not this time.

The two were as high as they could be, yet they seemed to sense a change in the air. Both of these boys were old hands at this office routine, and something was different this time.

Nancy looked at them and instructed them to go wait in the hall; she'd call them back in a few minutes. The two of them walked out of the office and took chairs along the wall where the bad children usually sat while the Vice-Principal called their homes. They looked at each other, and LD said, "I think she's calling home?" How wrong he was.

ZJ looked at him with an expression of questioning on his face, shrugged his shoulders, and then replied, "Who cares?"

A few minutes passed, then LD looked at ZJ and gave him a shove on the arm, "Hey, look man, this could be alright. We get detention; we score some sales; Big Guy is happy, and we get laid for free, right?"

ZJ was not really listening, and he replied, "Yeah, you could be right."

Nancy came over to the two, looked at her office door, and tilted her head in a 'Get in there' gesture. The two boys got up and trudged into Nancy's office only to be met by Dr. Fritz. ZJ looked at Fritz without respect for him or for the position he held and blurted out, "What?"

Fritz was not amused, nor was he in the mood to play word games, so this was going to be a bit tricky. He needed the two boys to do some serious lying for him.

He looked at LD and informed him, "You're going to Saturday School. Now get out of here."

The two boys both stood up, but Fritz looked ZJ right in the eye and clarified, "Not you; you stay, and LD, you can close the door on your way out. Nancy, write up the Saturday detention for LD and get him back to class."

Once LD was gone, Fritz started in on ZJ, "I know it's not your real name, but for right now, I'll call you ZJ. Are you high right now, ZJ?" Fritz demanded. Without waiting for an answer, he started in again, "If you don't tell me the truth, I will have an officer take you to the hospital and have a blood test done. Now, are you high?"

"What happens if I am?" ZJ offered.

"Well, now we're getting to a point of agreement, aren't we?" Fritz thought that he was pretty smart.

"Yeah, well, I guess. What do you want?" ZJ was guessing that something was up.

"I want you to come back to school sober, and when you get here, I want you in my office —— straight. Got It?" Fritz was all but yelling.

Socrates, the philosopher, was known to have said, "Justice was reward to your friends and the delivery of war upon your enemies." ZJ had just become a pawn in an ancient game where justice was going to fit his circumstances. He just didn't know how poetic justice worked yet, or *any* kind of justice for that matter.

Chapter 13

The Accusation

The day ZJ and LD were sent to the office, I was also called down to the office. I wasn't positive that it had to do with the morning confrontation with ZJ and LD, but I knew it was highly likely. I couldn't ignore the summons, as that would have been insubordination. Insubordinate, I'm not.

I knew I should get union representation, but I was still naïve enough to believe that I could handle my own affairs. I really didn't believe that such highly educated people could be as ruthless as this crew was. How do you get a degree at the PhD level and still be dishonest. This was a school and this was education, not commerce or industry. This place was not west of the Pecos River, and this could not be Judge Roy Bean style justice. Well, I was wrong, and it would be.

As I approached Dr. Fritz's office, the silence in his office could be heard a mile away. It was spooky. I knocked on the open door.

"Take a seat," Fritz was real businesslike today.

I knew something was up, since most the times I had been ordered to come in there, there had been no invitation to be seated.

The next sentence should have never been uttered by any schoolman, anywhere in the world, at any time throughout history, but, by God Almighty, there it was.

I had been chosen by the life force to deal with it.

"What a crappy teacher you are," was delivered matter-of-factly by Dr. Fritz.

This was a declaration of war, and Fritz knew it. He waited for a reaction.

When after a few seconds he got no reaction, he went on, "You think you're so glib and witty, and then you go and pull a boner like this." I kept my silence. My poker face was in place, and I didn't move a muscle. Feeling that he had the upper hand, "You jerk!" came out of his mouth with bluster and bravado. He was being as cavalier as he could be.

My brilliant reaction was, "What did you say?"

"You heard me, you jerk! I never wanted you in my school, and you can believe me that I have a file on you a mile thick, but with this one, I should be able to get you fired, you jerk!" He really liked calling me a jerk, as if it was a bullet that he kept firing at me from point-blank range.

He kept waiting for the emotional blow-up that he needed to get me to say things he could use against me. Instead, I stood up and said, "This stops right here. Call me back when the union rep is here."

"You would run, you lousy asshole. Hiding behind your Mama's big, union skirt," he was enjoying himself now. He thought he had me. This was the moment he loved, the moment when his vulgarity was hidden from public view. He could usually get the other person to sink to his level. This was the moment of truth for him, and he was getting excited, really excited.

"Sit down, you asshole!" he yelled as loudly as he could, and with no consideration or restraint. The door was open and the staff in the office was tuned in. This must have been like tuning in to the afternoon soap opera for them.

I knew he couldn't keep me here once I asked for a union rep, but he sensed my rage and was going for broke.

"Look, jerk!" he yelled again so loudly that I think I actually heard one of the office staff chuckle. At least I was back to jerk, down on the scale from asshole. I couldn't restrain myself, and I actually started to laugh. This was like a scene from out of an old episode of *MASH*. He was looking really foolish, and I wasn't biting at the bait.

I said, "It looks like I have been demoted." He didn't get it. No, I really mean it; he just didn't get it. It flashed through my head that I was Hawkeye, and he was Frank Burns playing the general.

"You aren't leaving here until I say you can," he yelled, not knowing what to do with the jab.

I just started to walk out.

"You provoked a student into doing things he shouldn't have done, so go and get your union rep and then come back. I own you, asshole!"

"Oh well, we're back to asshole." I wasn't getting very far. I looked at him, and with a grin on my face, I asked, "Promoted, huh?" He didn't get it; really, he didn't. I couldn't believe that he didn't get it. I'm still amazed, to this day, that he wasn't tuned in enough, or bright enough, to get it. I walked out, really amused at the ridiculous exchange that had just taken place. The humor was one-sided, I assure you.

I walked into Denny's classroom. He was the teachers' union rep.

"Denny, I need you to go to the office with me, right now." I was still amused, but trying not to show it.

Denny was in the middle of a class, but he could tell that he was needed. This wasn't the first time that this had happened.

We stepped outside the classroom and he asked, "What happened now?" So I recounted the tale.

Denny looked at me and asked, "How was it that you didn't loose it in there, and what the hell were you doing in there alone in the first place?"

I just looked at him and said, "I don't know, but I've got a problem now."

"Not as big a problem as you would have if you had said something that would fry you," Denny explained. Again, he looked me straight in the eyes and said, "You ain't bullshitting me, are you? Because if we get in there and it isn't exactly as you have said, we're in for trouble."

Denny got on the phone and made some arrangements with a hall monitor to watch his class, and off to the office we went. As he talked to himself in some preparatory, under-the-breath whisper, I could hear Denny saying, "He's up to his old tricks."

We arrived at the office and walked in.

"Denny, it's so good to see you," the phony son-of-a bitch said.

Fritz was now a totally different person than he was a moment ago.

"We're here to see you about a meeting you just had with P," Denny was being dead serious.

"Oh, and what's the problem?" Fritz's innocent act was making me sick.

"P seems to think that calling him an asshole isn't very professional," Denny wasn't joking when he said it.

"Well, as you know, Dennis, I have no idea what you're talking about, and neither does anyone else," again, Fritz displayed his cavalier attitude.

"Then what was your meeting about?" Denny was puzzled.

"We have a student who claims that Mr. P provoked

him into an act of anger." Fritz was setting me up.

"Did the student threaten Mr. P, Dr. Fritz?" The inquiry was a legitimate question.

"He may have." Fritz started to hedge his bet, since he didn't know what the students would say.

"When will we know?" Denny was trying to nail Fritz down.

"We will know as soon as we get the students' statements," again, hedging the bet.

"We want to have a union rep present when you talk to the students." Denny wanted to prevent a fabrication of the story.

"We'll see," Dr. Fritz was noncommittal.

"Are you issuing a formal reprimand; are you leveling a charge at P?" Denny was trying to get this incident watered down to something he could counter.

"That remains to be seen," Fritz was now becoming ridiculous again.

Denny looked at me and said, "You are not to go near Dr. Fritz or his office without me or the other union rep, Sue. Got it?"

We left the office and Denny went down the hall to his room, while I went down a separate hall. As I walked down those terrazzo surfaced halls, through the fire doors, and into my classroom, I was transcendent of time. I felt like that little kid struggling against the teachers, administrators, and the prejudices of another era. It was like 1960 all over again.

Chapter 14

The Deal

ZJ was in Dr. Fritz's office first thing the next morning. He was hung-over from a lack of sleep, not to mention the drugs that were well on their way to wearing off. He was emotionally shot, irritable, and pissed that today he had to be as close to sober as he had been in the last two years. Fifteen-years-old and he was hooked on cocaine, crack, and sometimes he used methamphetamines to get him through the days when he couldn't get his drug of choice. ZJ was smart, hooked, and had a mom that was in total denial. ZJ knew she wanted to remain that way. What was Fritz going to do to him? He really didn't care.

Fritz was, himself, hung-over from the beer and Canadian Club whiskey that he had submerged his conscience in. Liquor was his god. It gave him the courage to face the next day. In fact, it had given him the sleep that he needed to live. Fritz was a smart drunk, never driving or being in public while intoxicated. He knew it was under control. He was no drunk. He could quit anytime he wanted.

"ZJ, I need your attention," Fritz demanded.

"What?" the defiant ZJ retorted.

"ZJ, you're at Northwest High because I allow you to be here," Fritz was laying out the threat.

"What?" ZJ replied as if to question.

"I want to call your mom in for a sit down," another threat. Fritz was testing for a reaction. After twenty-five years of being around kids, he knew he could find the reaction he was looking for if he tested the emotional landscape long enough. He was dealing with a young, hung-over junkie. He also knew that ZJ had a lot to hide and a lot to be ashamed of. But most important of all, a lot of guilt to carry.

ZJ knew he was one of the best con artists that had ever been born. He had his mom deceived, so why not play this jerk, too. It seemed that the only person that he couldn't deceive was the Big Guy, his pusher, and the owner of his soul.

"Yeah, go ahead and call Mom, get her down here and you will meet Mom and Steve," he was issuing a threat. This was looking like two dogs growling at each other.

"Who's Steve?" asked Fritz, impressed by the brass balls on this kid.

"Steve, the mouthpiece, the delivery man of noise, of pressure, and fear, the lawyer," ZJ was defiant and rebellious.

"I don't get it. Are you making a threat?"

"I'm makin' a promise."

Fritz now looked a bit surprised at the quickness of the answer, and ZJ looked a little bit irritated that he hadn't evoked a more emotional response. If he can get Fritz to blow up, he wins. ZJ knew how to get to you and render you neutral. He was well schooled in these street tactics because he had run with junkies and addicts that would steal the shirt off your back if it meant more drugs. He was one of the best at getting you mad and creating the diversion that was necessary to draw your attention away from your goal. He would keep at it long enough to confuse you, thus allowing a person to survive in the street jungle.

The world that a junkie lives in is one that is full of tactics that are not governed by civil law. The drug trade is, after all, the most free of free markets, with no laws or courts, and where "Survival of the fittest" and "Might makes right" are the only laws. The rules are simple; those who adapt will live, and those who fail to adapt will die.

Fritz wasn't going anyplace but where he wanted, so he stood up from behind the big, oak desk and pulled a chair up close and personal, eyeball to eyeball with ZJ. Dressed in his three-piece-suit, and with impeccable hygiene, Fritz was an impressive force.

That was, until ZJ caught that, ever so subtle, odor of alcohol on Fritz's breathe. ZJ knew, from that moment on, whom Fritz worshiped; John Barleycorn was Fritz's god. Fritz was self-medicating, as they would say in clinical circles. To ZJ, it was an avenue to control, and he couldn't wait to tell Big Guy.

"Look, you punk, we're going to come to an understanding. I know what you do and who you work for. I know a lot more than you think I know, punk. You're going to work for me and for Big Guy. Yeah, that's right, you punk. I know what you do and who you work for; do I need to repeat it again?

"You are going to do just as I tell you. You will be allowed to remain at this school with all that it may mean to you and to Big Guy. Do you think I don't know who sells and who uses? Do you think I don't read the police reports?" Fritz was laying it out for ZJ.

ZJ was taken aback by the speech, but it still hadn't sunk in yet. He was surprised to find out that Fritz knew more than he'd thought.

"You little punk, I own you just like Big Guy does, and you don't even know it. You punk, you just don't get it, I own you, now repeat after me, 'Yes, sir, Dr. Fritz.' Say it, you punk, 'Yes, sir, Dr. Fritz.' Say It." Fritz was now yelling. He was cold, ruthless, and totally without compassion for anyone or anything, and he was especially without any caring for this young junkie.

"Yes, sir, Dr. Fritz," ZJ said with no conviction, in a low tone, testing Fritz's resolve.

"Again, you asshole," Fritz whispered in his ear.

"Yes, sir, Dr. Fritz," ZJ repeated with a low volume.

"Again!" Fritz demanded, louder.

"Yes, sir, Dr. Fritz!" this time said with a military snap and cadence to it.

"You are going to do exactly what I say, or you are going to wish you had never met me. I own you, punk. I will be respected by you, now and forever. You think I'm kidding? Well, you won't after tonight, because you're going to get a beating, not one that will kill you, but one you will not soon forget. I know you don't believe me, yet, but you will —— I promise you." Of course, Fritz was bluffing, and ZJ didn't know it yet, but Fritz was closer to the truth then he realized.

Now ZJ was mad. He was also a kid. His emotions were right near the surface. It was easy for him to be led into an emotional rage, since he didn't have the years of annealing that it takes to get to Fritz's level of disrespect for his fellow human beings.

"You jerk!" ZJ countered. "How do you know that I'm not packin' after I leave here? How do you know someone ain't got my back? Try it, jerk, and your guy might end up dead!" ZJ was firing back with the flash and the posturing of false bravery.

Big words for a junkie, a small-time junkie trying to be tough, but ZJ knew Big Guy would keep his star player on the field as long as he was producing the green. He had been threatened before, and by those tougher than this drunk playing high school god and principal. Humoring this jerk was about to end, because ZJ realized that he just needed to get to Big Guy and find out what to do.

ZJ stood up and flicked Dr. Fritz "The Bird" as he walked out.

After Fritz could no longer see ZJ, he took a deep breath, slowly exhaled, and said under his breath, "Got you, punk."

Dr. Fritz went home that evening, put three ice cubes in a lowball glass, and poured out the amber colored liquid that he worshiped. He knew the problems of the day would melt with the ice as the whiskey took effect.

Chapter 15

Big Guy

Just like every evening, ZJ and LD put aside the events of the day and were all business. It was time for the evening deliveries. The deals in school had been made, and the marketplace had once again been fruitful. Everything Big Guy had taught them about the teenage drug trade had paid off. Now it was time to collect. It was time to go to work.

First, they would go to Big Guy's apartment for a line or two to make the shakes go away; it also helped in the courage department. Then, they would need a little extra dope to help get laid after the deliveries have been made. Now, down to the business at hand, dope deliveries.

Big Guy, like LD and ZJ, was also a middleman in the chain of distribution; he was hoping to move up soon, as he was aware that the level he was at was a high-risk endeavor. The biggest risk is in dealing dope to teenagers. Unlike adult users, their hardened counterparts, teenage junkies tattle the minute that they get caught. Unlike ZJ and LD, Big Guy was not a junkie. He had "Kicked" a long time ago. This was unusual in the dope business, but Big Guy was in it for the money. He had plans for moving up in this organization to which he was loyal. He was also an anomaly in the business, in as much as he was a fifteen-year veteran of narcotics anonymous and was a trained drug counselor. These were nice credentials for a drug outlaw. He clearly understood the drug user, and he clearly understood the disease of addiction and its pathology.

He lived in a middle-class apartment on the east side of St. Paul in an area of urban decline. An exiting white population had hit this area of St. Paul hard. The east side of St. Paul was being replaced by a middle-class group of diverse, ethnic populations.

The area was not covered by graffiti yet, but the strip malls were being closed, and the check-cashing stores were everywhere. Pawnshops were fast replacing the hardware stores and the other storefront businesses that had been all up and down White Bear Ave. in the sixties and seventies. The remnants of the blue-collar class housing that had dominated this residential area in the '50s was still the prevalent real estate. What dominated the neighborhood was the housing industry's eight hundred square foot, rambler home with a detached garage and an alley out back.

The tree-covered streets were still there. The retired, blue-collar workers who had not left their paid-off homes had stayed, but only out of necessity. The elements of a well cared for neighborhood were still there. The lawns were cut; the sidewalks were edged, and the hedges were neatly clipped.

Even the newcomers were trying to maintain the value in their real estate. Everyone tried hard to keep up with the old traditions of a middleclass home, yet the tensions between races were there. The newcomers brought with them the tools of upward mobility, ghetto style, just hidden a little bit better in their new neighborhood.

Big Guy's apartment, at one time, had been a top of the line apartment. When it was built back in the sixties, it had been built to withstand the years, and it was still nice forty years later. The walls were plaster and the trim was oak; The halls had been laid with new carpet sometime in the '70s; The windows were old but nice; The place was still well taken care of, just older. Big Guy felt comfortable in the neighborhood, yet he didn't stand out.

It was just what he wanted, to run his drug franchise out of his home and be as inconspicuous as possible. The carpet was laid over oak floors, and the ranch oak trim had not been painted in apartment number eight, on the second floor, Big Guy's home *and* place of business.

Big Guy went to the door when the two young junkies showed up. He knew who was there but still looked through the peephole.

"Fuckin' A, man," ZJ said as they walked into the apartment's living room. There was a nice couch, a love seat which was set at an angle, a single chair, and a large, glass coffee table in front of the couch. The stereo system was playing some music which was strange to the boys' ears. The classical music made it seem like a grandma's home, and not the choice of music for a dealer, especially one as successful as Big Guy.

"Fucking A, what's happenin', dawgs?" Big Guy fired back at ZJ.

"We had a weird day, Big Guy," ZJ chimed in.

"I heard." Big Guy knew everything that happened at Northwest High and other schools that were in his territory.

"How did you know?" ZJ really was curious.

"I know everything that happens at that school," Big Guy's tone was almost scolding.

"We had a fucking, weird, office visit, Big Guy," LD added, "or, I should say, ZJ had a weird office visit."

"Tell me in your own words what happened, and don't leave anything out," Big Guy still sounded irritated. He had taught these boys to only disrupt enough to get themselves included in the bad boys group, but not enough to get real attention. These two had crossed the line. They needed to reform. They had gotten themselves thrown out of the drug buying groups at their old school. He'd had to start them all over at this new school, and they weren't doing so well at Northwest, either.

ZJ told the story and about the deal that Fritz had mentioned in his office, "He really wants us to get P," ZJ related to him. This really worried Big Guy, but he decided to drop the irritated attitude because he was now thinking about something else. What he was thinking about would have to be covered at another level above him. He didn't want to alarm these two boys. Anyway, they had a big night ahead of them.

"You two are not only going to deliver your day's sales, but I have arranged for you to deliver another junkie's sales for today."

This was dangerous, both for the drug representatives, who in this case were ZJ and LD, and for the customers. There were unknowns for the drug users, and these were untested waters with risk for both. No one knew what would happen when people that ZJ and LD didn't know started collecting money and delivering expensive inventory. The customers were, after all, people addicted to drugs with no goals in their lives other than to obtain drugs. Big Guy said it was necessary, so the two would have to do what they were told; anyway, Big Guy owned these two, so they would do whatever they were told, regardless of the risk.

Big Guy went over to his computer, and at his

urging, an expensive laser printer started printing labels with the weight in grams and a coded substance identified on the label as powdered milk, baby powder, vitamin tablets, etc. These substances were really crack, heroin, cocaine, or whatever the customer had ordered. The names on the labels, however, were of everyday, common substances. The records were carefully kept, as Big Guy was very sophisticated and knew that if he got caught, the records might be a valuable chip in a plea bargain. If he could avoid getting caught, he had very good records of collections and marketing lists that formed a database for marketing campaigns.

On many occasions, he had sent a new salesman to an old customer who had been ripped off by one of his other salesmen. He had the locations of the sales. He had the real names of his customers. He had the advantage in the fact that his customers didn't even know he existed. He was an abstract concept to most users. He could just send a new salesman to an old customer after a junkie got pissed at his regular pusher. Big Guy was good at what he did and was expanding his sales base with the efficiency that only an automated computer system could give him.

He knew who used what and how often they needed it. He even knew the important, well-connected people who used drugs and what kind of pusher could approach them. He was good at what he did.

Hell, he had even thought about running a sale to increase volume, but he usually ended up laughing at himself when he got the idea that he was running a legitimate business. He was a realist to a fault, taking no risks without checking with his supervisor before he acted. It had worked for years, and he was handling the biggest territory in the northern suburbs. He would tell himself, Just a few more years, and I'll be out anyway. I'm real close to retirement, and then, on to St. Croix in the Caribbean and a life of ease.

Big Guy counted out the bags, and then put a printed, pressure sensitive label on each bag. The computer started printing a re-order list for his "Just in time" inventory system. He was keeping a minimum of drugs in his apartment at all times. He prided himself on being as good at the drug retail business as Wal-Mart was at selling consumer goods. This was a well-educated, well-read executive. ZJ and LD didn't have any idea how dedicated he was.

Big Guy looked at ZJ and LD, smiled, laughed, and then said, "It's party time. You two are going to be rich after tonight. Your commission will be close to $2,300. That means you will have to get back to me with twenty three thousand bucks before you call it an evening. Hey, why don't you two pay me now, and then you can charge anything you want and use what's leftover on chicks." Big Guy knew darn well that these two had spent every penny they'd ever had. He was just making fun of them. He really enjoyed this part of his job.

"Hey, ZJ, your last stop of the day is a new drop at the hockey arena where you will find a hockey player who needs help. He needs the green label pills, a new item which might turn out to be a big seller." Steroids were new to Big Guy, but they were selling well to a new market, athletes.

Big Guy told ZJ and LD, "This is a new drug that will make you big and strong. This could be a mega market for you two, if you could just get to know the jocks." If ZJ had only known what was really going on and what had been planed for him that evening, the Fates may have been cheated by his reaction.

Big Guy laid out a small amount of white powder

on the glass-topped coffee table. He handed both the young junkies razorblades and looked at both of them, laughing, "Fight for your supper, you two dawgs." LD let ZJ take the first line that he cut from the pile. LD always knew that ZJ would split the dope fairly between the two of them. LD knew that his friend and classmate since kindergarten would do what was right.

Chapter 16

The Cave

ZJ and LD knew that they had some new users on the evening route. This was a good time. The first time that they sold drugs to new users, they got to sample the goods. It was an act of faith on the pusher's part to use with the new client. This was a sales technique that had a history of proven results. If there were any chicks in the crowd of new users, ZJ and LD would party with them until the drugs were ingested, shot, or smoked.

Big Guy knew that he would never tap into the disease of addiction until and unless he introduced the addicts to their new god. This new god was not benevolent; it was one that would consume the individual and produce a stream of revenue to the dealer for years to come, and the younger, the better. Because the longer a junkie used drugs, the longer Big Guy had a customer. There was a high turnover rate because addicts tend to die early in life.

Parents are also very naive about their young children. They believe that they still have children at home. Middle school is the best shot Big Guy had at starting kids on drugs. LD and ZJ had been top producers in middle school. Now, as high school drug reps, they had not been the best he'd ever had. They were still producing, but Big Guy thought that maybe they had become complacent. The two had been the best in middle school. Here they were, only fifteen and already over the hill. Big Guy was thinking that it was time to turn them into customers and retire them from sales.

Before the two had left the apartment, and after the two had sampled the goods, ZJ and LD were getting ready to leave for the appointed rounds.

Big Guy looked ZJ straight in the eye, laughed out loud, and said, "ZJ, just remember, on some days, the bear gets the hunter, and on some days, the hunter gets the bear." Big Guy was toying with ZJ, and ZJ was not sophisticated or experienced enough to realize that Big Guy was laughing at him. "Be careful, ZJ, tonight may be the night the bear gets you." Big Guy was really getting a kick out of taunting ZJ.

"Yeah, what?" ZJ was in a drug haze but was intuitive enough to realize that he was suppose to have gotten something out of the lesson that Big Guy was teaching. Just like all the lessons that ZJ was supposed to have learned, this one was a wasted lesson in a drugged mind.

"Yeah, know the situation, ZJ? Remember, be on your toes; the drug drop can turn on you and go bad in a heartbeat. Always beware of the cave, the one where the mad bear lives, because you cannot tell what the bear is protecting, or what it is willing to do to achieve its goals. Don't tangle with a mad bear, and don't let the bear get you." It was a warning, and it would to go unheeded.

All this time, Big Guy is laughing and joking, making light of the task at hand yet warning of the inherent risk that existed in the evening to come. He was remembering back to his own youth, and how at fifteen he had been immortal. He was remembering how drugs had ruined his life and wandering down the road of regrets and lost loves. He was longing for the girl that had walked away from him and his disease. What might his life have been like? If only —— then he stopped himself. He was entering a place that he used to fix with drugs and beer. In an attempt to get the girl back, he found sobriety. But it was too late; she wouldn't take the risk on him and it was over. He was in a place he didn't want to be. He had to rely on his AA training to change his thinking pattern.

He then refocused on the home in the Caribbean he would soon have. He thought about the life that he would lead as soon as he had just a little more money. He was also in the presence of two young junkies he was sure wouldn't see twenty. This quickly brought his attention back to the here and now.

Here were these two punks that had sold their souls, and were, in fact, owned by another. All this had happened because of their youthful passion for sex, excitement, and self-aggrandizement. They were led into addiction, eager for the fast life, and what they got, they had wished for.

Neither one ever understood the warning that Big Guy had issued. When you're that age, the only way you learn is by failing and paying the price for failure. It would be so for these two.

The two boys left the company of Big Guy, high and loaded down with enough drugs to put any adult in prison for forty years. If caught, these two boys would do no time at all, as they would be first-time drug offenders.

The events of the night went without complication. The two boys partied with several new customers, and they had some fun with a couple of young, female addicts who paid more than money for their drugs. The deliveries were made and the money was collected.

Now, it was time to go to the hockey arena and meet another new customer.

The only clue to who this new junkie could be was on the printed computer label. They were to ask for the "Hockey player," then, Hockey player's response should be, "Things go better with coke."

The Hockey arena was like a thousand other hockey arenas across the country. Built with American Legion money, collected from the sale of pull-tabs in the local bars, it was a well-kept facility. At night, with the lights turned on and the parking lot well lit, this was a place that had held the dreams of many a high school hockey player, thinking that he was just a few games away from the big leagues.

Everyone at Northwest knew that ZJ and LD were the go-to guys for drugs, so just their presence at the hockey arena was disturbing to the hockey players and the young ladies that had come to watch them. As LD and ZJ split up, they started looking for the one they were to call, Hockey player.

As ZJ went around to the players' entrance, he recognized a classmate from my classroom, "Hey, what's up, man?" Maybe it was time to square up the debt for "Ratting" on him in my classroom. ZJ was famous for never missing an opportunity to bully someone.

"Nothing," replied Hank.

"Just hangin', man?" ZJ was toying with Hank. He had no idea how to treat people.

Intuitively, Hank made eye contact with ZJ and fired off a preemptive communication, "Look, ZJ, I'm not the one you're looking for." Hank was thinking that ZJ was trying to sell him drugs, but ZJ was going about the task of picking a fight.

Hank wasn't sure what ZJ wanted, but he waited until ZJ was starting for him and then called out, "ZJ."

Hank was not totally sure what he was going to say. What he was about to say would even surprise him, so he paused to think. The pause was read by ZJ to be a sign of weakness. ZJ turned to look for LD. He needed LD to make sure that he won the fight.

Hank spoke with incredible clarity, "ZJ, you're in Mr. P's class with me, and I don't like the crap you've been giving him, so cut it out."

This really amused ZJ. In fact, he started laughing. The laughing became irrational. The sincerity with which Hank had spoken was not something that ZJ, the bully of middle school, had ever seen before. *What the hell*, thought ZJ. *This asshole just doesn't get it; you don't screw with me. I can still intimidate this little prick, just like I did when we were in middle school.*

ZJ finally quit laughing like a crazy man. What he then said was not funny to anyone, especially not Hank. "Look, asshole, I do as I please in every class. If P wants to take me on, I'm ready for him. If you think that some weak, punk-ass, wanna-be tough guy like you is gonna tell me who to leave alone and who to fuck with, your ass is grass. So get the fuck over to the candy store with the other little boys, or go home and tell your mama what a bad boy I am, but don't ever get in my face again, dick-head!" ZJ was so eloquent and respectful.

Hank just looked at him, not saying a word.

ZJ was closing the distance between them, fully expecting Hank to turn and run at any second. ZJ came closer, and closer, until he was right in Hank's face. ZJ started yelling, "Asshole! Asshole! Asshole!" ZJ was so close that Hank could smell the chemical stink on ZJ's breath, in fact, he could smell a combination of tobacco, alcohol, and chemicals that were being processed by ZJ's respiratory system in an attempt to rid itself of the unwanted substances in his system. This was not endearing to Hank who stood his ground, never saying a word. He just stood there, staring at ZJ.

All this didn't go unnoticed by Hank's teammates and friends, as they started to gather around Hank. Within seconds, Hank was joined by teammates, hockey players, and spectators, and many had hockey sticks. ZJ, no stranger to a fight, especially an unfair fight, started to be aware of the numbers of loyal mates that Hank had gathered. ZJ didn't have his group with him. ZJ didn't even have a group. He was also jealous of Hank and the loyalty that his friends and teammates were displaying.

He realized that even LD was nowhere to be seen. He eventually backed away, but not without a few last words, "Look asshole, your friends can't be around you forever. Just remember, you don't fuck with superman, Leroy Brown, or ZJ." ZJ turned and walked away, something he would not have done if the tables had been turned. These were not street fighters, junkies, or pushers; they were just kids trying to help a friend. ZJ wasn't laughing anymore.

A few minutes later, and a safe distance away from Hank and his friends, LD walked up to ZJ and said, "I found Hockey player and we've had the best day ever. Let's get this long green back to Big Guy. We'll get our stuff, find some bitches, get laid, and get wrecked one more time before we go home."

"Yeah," was all ZJ could muster, as he turned his attention to the bag of green that he and LD had collected. It held twenty-three thousand bucks, big dough for these two street punks. LD started yelling, "Yeah, a lot of green! A lot of green!"

ZJ started smiling, and his thoughts turned to the drugs and women that this kind of money would secure for him and LD.

Chapter 17

The Sting

LD started walking to the car, away from the ballpark and into the parking lot, but ZJ lingered for a second to see if he had anything to worry about and kept looking back at the hockey arena. As ZJ picked up the pace to catch up to LD, the lights of the hockey arena began to fade, and the parking lot came into sight. There were cones of light raining down from the light poles, with rings of light drifting down onto the blacktop. The night was clear and cloudless. This evening would have been perfect, but for the events that were about to unfold.

As the two caught up to each other in the parking lot, a kid with a dark, hooded sweatshirt, blue jeans, and smooth black shoes came up behind them. It was as if a ghost had appeared out of the dark between the lighted areas of the parking lot. Neither one of the two had even sensed the presence of this silent, small person. ZJ heard a small voice, something that stopped him cold.

"Say what, LD?" ZJ hoped he'd heard LD.

"What, ZJ?" LD hadn't heard a thing.

Everything changed in the split second that it took for ZJ to reach for his car keys. ZJ didn't have a license, but of all his indiscretions, driving without even a permit was just a minor point.

"If either one of you wants to see tomorrow, you better do exactly what I say," the voice from Hell had spoken. It wasn't loud or demanding; it was just there.

Both dealers were totally taken by surprise. They spun around and looked at a pair of eerie eyes, the kind that the Goth kids wore to make themselves look weird. Worse yet, the eye coverings were luminescent and glowed in the dark.

"If you reach for a weapon, you're dead," a cool calm voice stated. The voice was coming out of the hooded sweatshirt standing about six feet away. In the dark light of the parking lot, the figure looked almost comical. The not so funny part was that he had a pistol pointed right at them.

He was all made up with dark eye shadow, eye inserts, and black, theatrical face paint framed his face in the outline of the pullover hood. ZJ and LD could hardly see the flat, black, .22-caliber handgun with a matt finish, as it was held in a hand gloved in a dark purple, rubber surgical glove. For a split second, the two were all but giddy looking at the attire of their adversary. A feeling that was short lived.

It took them but a nanosecond to realize that the pistol had a silencer on the muzzle of the barrel.

All of a sudden, the gun with its muzzle swollen by the silencer looked huge. Not much went on for the moment that it took for LD to realize that this may be the end of the ride. In some strange way, he was actually feeling relief, and not what one would expect.

The voice was weak and small and as flat as the matt finish on the gun, "If you two would please turn over your car keys?" This came from the strange, small figure with the long sleeved, hooded sweatshirt with the great big gun pointed at them.

It's funny how sober you can become when you

need to, thought ZJ. This was a simple carjacking and nothing to worry about. He didn't want the sweat soaked jockstrap that LD was transporting in a gym bag. A gym bag at hockey arena could only contain hockey gear, right, ZJ rationalized to himself. The car was all this guy was after.

How could he know what was in the gym bag?

"Want to jack the car? Here, take the keys." ZJ whipped the keys down onto the pavement in front of this strange, little man. "But I'd better not ever catch you," ZJ warned with bravado and clenched teeth.

He could hear the simple "*Swoooosh*," like the sound you hear when you release compressed air from a tire, and then, the sensation of a burning, and the feeling of a liquid running down ZJ's arm, and finally, the red color on the sleeve of his shirt. He thought he might have felt pain, but the only pain was a burning sensation. It took a second, but he knew that he had been shot. He heard the bullet hit the car door behind him, and he knew that as long as he lived, he would always remember the thud of the bullet hitting the metal of the door.

"What the hell!" were his first words, as he looked this weird, little man in the funny eyes that had been used to conceal his real eyes. ZJ's eyes were like silver dollars, as wide open as they could get without them rolling right out of his head.

The little man began to speak, "If I'd wanted you dead, you would already be dead." There was no emotion in his voice, just information.

Again, the funny, little voice came out of this thing that had just shot ZJ, "Now, if either one of you wants to graduate, give me the money, all of it, and every last cent. Got it?"

ZJ thought he was tough, but this guy didn't seem

tough at all, it seemed as though he was a machine, just doing, not feeling. He was a lawn mower, a conveyor belt, just an appliance doing its work. ZJ was a bit numb to all of this because he was bleeding, but it did not escape LD's attention.

LD went limp and collapsed right on the spot, just like a wet rag. LD was out cold. As tough as he thought he was, as mean as he thought he was, and as mean as he had been to others, he was still just a kid. His pants were wet in the crouch, and the smell of human waste was in the air. This sent a cold shiver through ZJ, as he had never seen anyone react as LD had. He was also loosing blood and beginning to feel physically weak himself. ZJ, who had never had a spiritual thought in his life, found himself making covenants with God. He had never even thought about a Supreme Being in his fifteen years.

He was promising to get straight, clean, and sober if God would spare his life.

ZJ instinctively reached for the moneybag that LD had been carrying and bent down to get the money. He slid it around on the pavement, never even questioning how this strange, little guy knew he had a large amount of money, and he kicked the bag across the pavement to the hooded guy.

The hooded guy then said, "Give me the keys. Pick them up and give them to me, slowly, and no funny business." ZJ did as he was told. Then, hooded guy got into ZJ's car with the money and slowly drove into the night. If fact, he was so in control that he drove slowly, using the blinker as he left the parking lot, just like you or I would if we'd just left a McDonalds parking lot.

ZJ automatically called Big Guy on his cell phone. He explained what had happened and asked what to do?

Big Guy said, "Look, you have to call the police and tell them everything except the amount of money that was taken. Tell them about being carjacked and being shot, and do it right now. Don't worry about the money. I will help you track it down after you get treated for your gunshot wound. Get LD taken care of. Give the police a good description of the car; maybe they can help us find this guy."

911 was called and the police showed up. LD was revived, and ZJ was taken to Regions Hospital. His mother was called from the hospital and she was on her way, assured that her son would live.

As LD sat waiting for his parents to show up at the hospital, it occurred to him that he could have been killed. LD thought to himself, *This is it; it isn't drugs, girls, and fun anymore; it's time to get out. I could get straight and put a lot of distance between me and ZJ. I know that things are just not going to be the same ever again.*

If he had only known how right, really right, he was, he might have opened up to his parents. If he could have seen things in a crystal ball and predicted outcomes, as my mom had been able to do, I know he would have done things differently that night.

He didn't open up to the police that night. True to his childhood friend, he was not going to get ZJ in trouble. For LD, this whole incident was even more complicated than just not telling on ZJ. ZJ was his family. It was the only family he really had.

ZJ's mom showed up and he told her about the carjacking, but that was all. He got eight stitches, four in the front of his arm and four more in the back where the bullet had gone out. He also got some great pain medication by prescription. He would get to stay home for a few days and stay legally high for his recovery. Why the bullet had not shattered the bone and left him crippled for life was a mystery. The doctors were amazed at the small amount of damage the bullet had caused. ZJ seemed to have more luck than sense.

Shortly after the ten o'clock news, the doorbell rang at Big Guy's apartment. Big Guy looked out the peephole and opened the door. In walked a little man with a hooded sweatshirt. He handed Big Guy the gym bag full of money. Big Guy opened the moneybag, reached in, got out ten of the one hundred dollar bills, and handed them to the hooded guy. Hooded guy handed the handgun and silencer to Big Guy, and then he asked, "Is that all you need, Big Guy?"

"Get out of here," Big Guy ordered, as he grabbed the gun and silencer.

"Ok," was all he said, and hooded guy disappeared into the night.

Chapter 18

Hockey Hank

The news of ZJ's adventure went through the school like wildfire. Such a tale of violence and gunshot wounds would create a stir at any high school in the country. All the kids were anxious to tell me the tale, none more so than Hank, who had defended my honor just minutes before ZJ got shot. He felt himself a hero in some way, because he had stood up to this now famous thug.

The next day, I was standing in front of my classroom door, saying hi to kids and trying hard to match names with faces. I was waiting for class to begin, when Hank walked up to me and in an immature manner said, "You really care, don't cha?"

I asked, "About what?"

"About kids." Hank seemed surprised that I didn't know what he was talking about.

In a knee-jerk reaction, I answered, "Yes, I do."

I wasn't sure what to make of the exchange. It was out of place for what little I knew about Hank. I concluded that kids do a lot of strange things that I don't understand. This was one of them.

Hank went in and sat down next to a pretty, young lady he had met in my class. Her name was Brittany, a bright student that was in my class for only one reason; she liked the teacher. Well, also it was maybe because there were lots of boys in my room. She didn't care much for the subject matter. The two were talking about what seemed to be nothing, when I heard Hank say, "Brittany, I saw ZJ at the hockey arena last night, and I told him to lay off P. I meant it, too. I really like P." I was sure that was meant for my ears.

"I really like him, too, Hank, but remember, ZJ and LD are creeps, so you would be better off leaving them alone; P can take care of himself," Brittany advised Hank.

"Yeah, I know, Brit." Hank was not all that smooth with girls, but this one seemed different.

"Did you hear the gossip about ZJ and LD getting carjacked in the parking lot at the hockey arena?" Brit was full of the story and really wanted to tell someone. Hank was smart enough, and smitten enough, to just want to hear her voice, even if it was to hear a story he had heard before.

Hank just casually lied about hearing the story and said, "No, tell me. Whad ya hear?"

"The story I heard was that they got carjacked and ZJ got shot in the arm. He had eight stitches, they say." Brit went on and told the tale, maybe even adding a little drama that wasn't in the story she had heard. After she was done, there was a short pause as Hank took in what she had said.

Hank was a bit awkward at this impressing a girl thing, but most tenth graders are, and he was no different. As he calculated his response, the thought flashed through his mind that this girl was special, and maybe one that he could really like. "Wow, that will improve sales," was all Hank could think of to say, not wanting the conversation to end.

"What do you mean?" Brit was truly curious at this point.

"ZJ and LD will talk up the tale and embellish it. They will make themselves look tough," Hank was really angry as he said this.

"So what?" Brit didn't understand.

"It's drama, Brit. Just drama and gossip that is intended to create a story that makes them the center of the bad-guy universe. The better the story, the more the bad guys and girls will want to know them. They will be dangerous and hip, and that will be great for sales. They are going to sell more drugs than anyone else," Hank's anger wasn't hidden as he talked.

"Hank, you stay away, please?" Brit sounded honestly concerned.

Was that genuine concern that I heard, Hank was thinking. *I hope it was?*

"I will, Brit, but it pisses me off." He was really mad. He was immature, but he was smart enough to know that a lot of kids would be sucked into a life of drugs and all the baggage that went with that life. He knew that the first encounter with drugs was a choice; the rest of the experience would be made by an addicted mind with the disease removing any choice. He was experienced beyond his years when it came to the addict. He knew more than most tenth graders in this regard.

"Hank, class is starting. Just get to work and P will be pleased, I will be pleased, and you can keep that A that P said you're getting in his class, get it?" She found herself giving him advice that she normally wouldn't give to someone if she didn't care about him. It hit her right that minute that she liked this guy, really liked this guy. Wow!

I was taking roll by the time the exchange had taken place, and we were starting the computers and loading the drawings. Hank and Brit approached me.

Hank started the conversation with a question, "Do you know Swede, the old hockey coach?"

I had been asked questions like this before by hockey players who were curious about what had happened to this well liked and popular varsity coach. Swede was still in the district, teaching as he always had at a middle school. I knew him from my early days in the district when we met through a mutual friend and had even found some common ground on which to base a friendship. He was a great guy, and I understood why young people would like him. He was personable and a very good listener. He wasn't the world's best choice for win/losses when it came to coaching hockey, yet that didn't seem to matter to his players. They just plain liked and respected him.

I was a bit puzzled and asked Hank, "Why do you ask?"

Hank and Brit were both looking at each other, wondering which one should start the reply, with neither one being quite mature enough to know how to approach the subject with social grace. This subject would be off limits in any other classroom.

"Well, Brit and I were wondering if you had heard the reason why Swede was let go from his varsity coaching position." I had no idea where this was coming from. The talk in the school, all day, had been of the shooting on the evening before.

Why are we talking about a hockey coach? I was wise enough to know that I could do nothing about what I was about to hear. The two had opened up a dialogue that they had obviously discussed before.

"No, I don't know the reason that Swede was let go." But I was curious now, "Tell me, what do you think happened?" I had taken the bait. There was no turning back now.

"We think that Fritz canned him because he didn't win enough games," Hank spoke for both of them.

Both were nodding their heads in agreement. Now, I had opened a subject that would have met with an "I don't know; now get back to work" in any other classroom in the building. If I had known what was politically correct and what was good for me, I would have done the same thing. Instead, I went where I thought we could get some teaching done, hoping for a teachable moment, and asked of the two, "Want to tell me?" I then sat back, ready to listen to the story.

Hank went right into what he thought had happened, as if he knew the exact details. *In fact,* I thought, *given the amount of detail and knowledge he is showing about how athletics works in the high school, he is quite impressive.*

He was quite sophisticated in the politics of how the system worked. This story had obviously been told before. He had developed his position and was selling hard.

"The way we think this happened was that Fritz decided that having a .500 season was not good enough for his Eskimos, so he was determined to get rid of Swede. He knew that Swede had just moved to a new house, so he sent out a coaching contract for the hockey season that was to come to the old house. He knew that by the time the mail got forwarded, it would have expired according to the terms that he had written into the new contract. The minute that the time was up, he called Swede and had him come in to the office. He then fired him for not responding to the request for the new contract. Swede was furious, as it had not been done this way ever before. He told Fritz that he had always been given the courtesy of a phone call when he needed to be renewed. Fritz explained that the old athletic director was retired, and now, things were going to be done Fritz's way. Short of an all-out school board fight, he could accept the fact that he had been fired, or he could fight a losing battle with the board." That was Hank's story. He sat back in his chair, looked at Brit, and said, "It's so, P."

I know that there had been a problem with Swede. I knew he had left the head coaching position, but I had always thought that Swede decided that life was too short for all the hours he spent coaching. He decided that he would as gracefully as possible go back to teaching at the middle school for reasons of his own. He never shared his anger with me or the school board. He certainly could have and may yet, someday. My guess would be that he would share his story when he thought he had a fighting chance of winning.

Hank just got madder and madder each time he told this story. The new coach was not there to teach the basics of the game; he was there to win at all costs. This included cutting Northwest High students from the team, in favor of out of district students that had been recruited by the new coach. Many of those students had been on that team from before middle school. Hank was one of them that had been cut. He was crushed. As he thought about this his eyes began to tear up, and Britt stepped in to console him.

I told the two students, "Step out into the hallway to collect yourselves, and return when you're ready." This was a big risk for a teacher at Northwest High; it was also the right thing to do.

I was told later that the beginning of their dating relationship had started that day in the hall.

Chapter 19

Impulse

We had started class and I was working on something, when a student that had known me from back in our middle school years came to my desk. She had followed my classes, tying to get into them. She liked being in my room. She was certainly more of an artisan than a draftsperson, but she had found a way to express her creativity through the use of the computer, drawing program I was teaching. I was fine with that, since any talent was welcome in my room.

On this day, Stacy pulled up a chair next to my desk, "Mr. P?"

"Yes?" I should learn not to pay attention to kids. *I'm being sarcastic.*

"I've got to sign up for my junior-year classes, and —— would you help me?" She was asking me to help her make some of the decisions she was struggling with.

What a complement, I thought. *This was the moment every teacher waits for, the chance to influence the lives of students. In this case, one I liked, and one who had been a loyal friend as well as a good student.*

"What can I do for you?" I was pleased that I would have some influence.

"Well, I was thinking that I would like to spend some time at the Jr. College. Maybe attend some of the basic classes that everyone has to do in their first year of college. Some of the kids are telling me that I can get credit for my high school graduation requirements as well as college credit. Better yet, the kids that I talked to said that the school district had to pay for it. They said that no one at school would tell me about it, because the school didn't want to give up the money that they get from the state. The kids I talked to also said that the school doesn't want to send their best students to a college. Is that true?"

"Stacy, I had all three of my girls do exactly what you're talking about." I was telling her that I was impressed with her desire, and that I approved.

"How does it work?" she wanted to know.

So, I began to tell her, "The way you get credit for both college work and high school credit is . . ." and I went to great lengths to give her details and pointers that the school would not have given her. I then warned her that the school would try and talk her out of it.

It was wonderful having ZJ and LD gone from the room, while they were recovering from the ordeal they had gone though. Although, I imagined that their idea of recovery was the two of them getting high someplace and partying hardy. Conversation with Stacy could be very productive when students that demand all your time do not distract you.

Anyway, as a way of protecting myself from any further nonsense in the classroom, I had cameras installed by my best, electronics class wizards. It's unbelievable what a group of kids with a mission and twelve hundred dollars to play with can do to visually surveil every part of the room. This was also a reassuring thing to the kids, since they were even more familiar with the antics of ZJ and LD than I was.

Let's get back to Stacy's problem. I was just about to wind up with the big news, finally. I must have been on a roll, as I was talking as quickly as I could.

With every sentence came another reason to further this young lady's chances at going to college and high school at the same time. The best reason was that if she got some college, albeit at the high school level, I knew from past experience that the chances that she will continue her education would increase greatly.

Finally, I said, as a manor of speaking, and with a wink and a nod, "You didn't hear this from me." I knew that the unwritten rule in Fritz's school was that we didn't counsel students to use the post-secondary college program because it reduced our budget.

Worse yet, what if the smart kids found out that it was the best way for them to go? We would lose all our precious, academic over achievers. On top of all this, the old hands that had all the really smart kids would have to teach and deal with the middle-of-the-road kids. This was a real problem, as the older teachers have, by their own determination and seniority, the God-given right to deal with only the upper, college-bound kids.

The words, "You didn't hear this from me," hadn't even hit the floor when out of the hall came Fritz at full gait. And, within seconds, he was standing face to face with me. I mean face-to-face, in my personal space, bringing new meaning to the phrase, "Being in your face."

"Care to repeat that?" he was yelling at me in front of thirty students.

I must have turned a bright shade of red. I was very embarrassed for him. I was ashamed to be in the same room with this trailer-trash administrator. He thought himself a leader and was showing off. How could anybody be this rude? In a world where children do as we do, and not as we say, such deeds are the equivalent of reverse role modeling. Who would want their child to act like this?

Desperately, I tried to change the subject, "Look at what Emily is doing on the computer," and I pointed out the outstanding work one of my prize students was doing. For just a moment, he seemed to take the bait, realizing that what he had just done had violated the rules of conduct that most civilized people recognized as legitimate behavior.

Quickly, I said, "Look at the detail on Emily's drawing." The attention-getting ploy stopped working right there. Please believe me; at this point I had the attention of thirty students. The room went absolutely silent.

Fritz demanded, in a voice that was more siren than request, "What were you talking about with this young lady?"

I didn't say a word. Shocked and dismayed, I stood there looking like a teacher without pants, not knowing what to say.

He really began yelling now, "You were sitting next to this girl! What were you saying? What were you doing?"

Then he changed his tone, as he turned his attention to Stacy, "Do you need to see a female counselor, or Miss Nancy? I will take you right now? If you need a private moment with anyone, I will take you." He was selling the subtlety of the implication, as much as selling the idea, that he would be her protector. The classroom got the idea.

The intent was veiled, but even the kids got what he was after. He wanted this young lady to implicate me. He wanted her to imply that I had done, or said, something at that desk that would be inappropriate.

Stacy rather naively looked at him and said, "It's

okay, Dr. Fritz; Mr. P was talking about post secondary classes."

That wasn't what he wanted to hear. He turned to me, and I swear, there never has been, or ever will be, a look that was as frightening as the stare he gave me. He turned and left, and I knew that it wasn't over, but then, it never was... with him.

I had a reason to call Denny, the union rep., because what had happened would result in a follow-up by Fritz. I thought for sure that as mad as he had been that I was going to get the "C Me" note. It didn't happen, but I did go to see Denny.

Right after school, I went to see Denny. As I walked in the door, he looked at me, rolled his eyes, and said, "I already know; nothing is secret in this school, especially a visit from 'Der Furor.' I had Sue get a statement from Stacy, and she said that Fritz was way out of line."

"Denny, do you have any idea what it took to get back on task after his majesty was in the room?" My cynical tone was apparent.

"I can guess." Denny was being sympathetic, in a not *too* sympathetic way.

"Look, damn it, you don't have any idea how hard I had to work to get that class back on task. You have no idea of the questions I had to answer. It is not easy to tell kids that an attack on a teacher in the classroom is an okay thing; it's not easy to tell kids that what happened was really not a bad thing, when it really was. Kids aren't stupid. They knew exactly what was happening. They knew exactly what was going on. It took the rest of the hour to turn that around." I was really mad and scared. My anger was at the surface, and an ugly thing it was.

"Well, did you?" Denny inquired.

"Did I what?" I wasn't listening to Denny.

"Turn it around?" Denny already knew, but he needed time to think.

"Of course, I did." What a lame conversation. Denny knew that this shouldn't have happened.

"Look, Denny, I want to talk to that asshole's boss. I want to talk to the superintendent?" I was mad and wanted to exact revenge. I didn't believe that any sane individual would stand for behavior like this.

"I can do that." Denny wasn't real happy with me at this moment, as he knew that the superintendent would just back Fritz, and that would be the end of that. Then, Denny thought, *Well, maybe P should learn that lesson the hard way.*

Denny was right; I just wasn't listening to him. I went to see the superintendent, but it was not even worth the time it took to see him, and, sufficed to say, he patronized me. The superintendent told me that I was exaggerating the situation. There was no discussion, just a short conversation controlled by the "Super," who frankly didn't give a damn. He was so removed and insulated from the operation of the schools that he would not have recognized a problem if it had bitten him on the ass.

This is one of the reasons that superintendents don't last in large school districts. The turnover rate of superintendents also allows the Dr. Fritz's of the world to keep their jobs, as a new super will not fire a sitting principal. In our district, we always have a new superintendent.

To illustrate this, I bring to your attention the man that this superintendent replaced. The former superintendent was released from his post because of an indiscretion. He lost his job, and the board buried the incident with a "Golden parachute." He was bought off with an undisclosed amount of taxpayer money. You or I would have been labeled as a social pariah, and we would have had to deal with the incident for the rest of our lives.

This incident never even saw the light of day. The grocery store incident for a young frightened girl turned out to be a pattern for this man of exemplary, high moral standards. She would never forget what she saw that day. How we hire such individuals in the first place always amazes me, but that's schoolmen and how they interpret their culture.

I did, however, accomplish one thing. I really pissed off Fritz. I'm sure I was back to *asshole* when he thought about me.

Chapter 20

Reprisal

The summer came and went, and we returned to the campus of Northwest High. I had always looked forward to returning to school in the fall, but this year was different.

Over the summer, I had explored leaving my position at Northwest High. I would have to give up my salary; it was at the top of the scale. I would have to start over again in some other school district, at the bottom of the seniority list, at the bottom of the pay scale. I would be the first to be laid off in an enrollment downturn. I decided that I would stick it out until something else opened up in my school district where I would not give up my tenure. I returned to what had started to become my personal Hell.

Think about it for a moment. I was caught in a system that rewarded the teacher for longevity but gave you no way out if the personal conflicts became unbearable. Worse yet, the teachers are caught in a given district with no way to improve their lot in life other than to leave the profession.

Principals from Hell get to operate with impunity for the same reason. They know that teachers can't leave, so they have no incentive to improve anything that has to do with what happens in the classroom.

If teachers were mobile, with pay and benefits that

followed them, they would vote with their feet, leaving principals from Hell behind. This would allow for the marketplace to do its work. Districts wishing to improve would seek teachers with great ideas and improved classroom approaches. Principals that thought of themselves as dictators would soon find themselves out of a job.

Keeping a proven success in the classroom would be important, as you would retain the best teachers and the best principals. Fritz was operating in a closed system where he could get away with what would have been judged criminal in an open marketplace.

All the political pundits who want a free market solution really don't want a free market solution. Good teachers would become local celebrities and demand larger pay packages. What the hypocrisy of the pundits demands is a system that takes away the protections that are in the union contract. The system then replaces the tenure and due process with the ability to fire teachers at will. What we then attract are those educators who have no choice but to work under any conditions that an administration would impose. Good people don't work for nothing. Try attracting a nun to a life of service for the church. It's a tough sell, in the modern world.

Fritz was operating without transparency; what he did was done without supervision or oversight. The law did not govern him; the board was removed from the oversight because that chore was expected of the superintendent. He also had a superintendent trying to survive the initial first few years of his appointment. The situation was ripe for abuse.

Fritz had spent the summer planning his reprisal. It had consumed him. Nailing me was at the top of his list. It's very difficult to fire a tenured teacher, so the plan was to implicate me in a criminal enterprise or a sex scandal. I have seen teachers survive sex scandals, so my demise would have to be a criminal charge.

To help you understand what it was he had to do, I'll tell the tale of a janitor that he hated. This particular night custodian was filmed taking a can of gas out of the tractor shed one evening. The security cameras had captured, on film, the removal of the gas can, yet, like the famous eighteen minutes of the Nixon tapes, the return of the gas was lost, somehow.

"The removal of the gas can was theft," Fritz later shouted at the board meeting. During the hearing that was held to exonerate this twenty-year veteran of the school system, the half-truths and innuendos worked. Fritz's bullying and bribing of the board paid off. He got the guy fired.

Turns out, this can of gas was used to help this employee's father, also a retired school employee. His father, who suffered from early stage Alzheimer's, had let his tank go dry. He had run out of gas in front of the school, a block from his home and a block from the gas station. The gas can was used by the night custodian's father to go to the gas station were the gas can was filled and replaced in the shed. The film with the replacement of the gas was never shown to anyone, and, in fact, that piece of video mysteriously disappeared. This is Fritz in his world.

Fritz had the luxury of time and timing. He could work his manipulations and schemes all he wanted, or he could just wait for an opportunity to reveal itself.

The problem he had with me was, he had waited to long to get me. The kids really liked me and with that went the parents of the kids who also really liked me. The dreaded parents, the ones who actually elected school board members. The one thing he knew he could not do was raise the awareness of some community activist or certain community groups. They would threaten the board members' reelections. He had to get me, somehow, on a charge that would not be questioned or investigated by the community.

Fritz was also cognizant of the fact that appearance was as good as the act of misconduct, itself. He had, on other occasions, forced voluntary resignations, his personal favorite, by creating an illusion of criminal misconduct. Most teachers, fearing for their licenses to teach, will do most anything to protect the right to teach. Doctor Fritz had used this tactic very effectively with teachers he had wanted gone.

The teacher I replaced had been forced into leaving in this very same way. It had been so simple to do, as the teacher I replaced had been young and trusting to a fault. He had been recruited out of Jacksonville, Florida. He had come from a tough, inner city, Jacksonville school. This young teacher had a great sense of humor. A sense of the absurd was a real gift when working with the kids that he'd had to work with in Jacksonville. He'd used this sense of humor to disarm this population of kids that had seen every human tragedy known to man.

Drugs were everywhere in Jacksonville, and the teen pregnancy program was overbooked, and as an industrial arts teacher, he'd had the toughest of the tough in his classroom. His particular following were streetwise and raw kids from the inner-city ghetto. Their humor was not that of our Mid-western culture. He had a quick wit and a glib language style that had been developed in this Florida environment. He had to be on his toes all the time. One last thing about this young teacher: He was a good listener and let students know he cared, even when he disagreed with what they were doing. He was like me in that way. It works.

Fritz had regretted hiring him, as he would not tattle on other teachers. Fritz liked teachers who told on each other because it divided them, causing mistrust and open conflict. Fritz saw himself as the CEO of Education Inc., not as principal of a high school. He could rationalize anything he wanted to do without ever taking personal responsibility for anything. He was a classical politico.

This young teacher was kidding around in class and using that sense of humor that had been his friend back in Jacksonville. He'd drawn a simple picture on the blackboard of a robust woman bending over, a simple drawing. He then turned to the class and said, "YO-momma." The laughing was robust, as well.

The self-appointed correctness cop, a science teacher down the hall, heard the laughter, and was in the room gasping and criticizing in a nanosecond. This young teacher was in Fritz's office answering obscenity charges after he received a "C-Me" note.

The teacher was going to make a lecture out of this drawing and the comment he had made about that drawing, but he never got the chance. He had dared to take a risk, maybe even a risk he would never take again, but we will never know how the lecture would have gone, will we? Nor will we ever know what innovation he might have brought to the classroom. In this environment, bad moves are not tolerated... if, in fact, it was a bad move.

"Get into my office, right this minute!" Fritz was yelling as loudly as he could.

The scene was as predictable as could be. Fritz started yelling at this Masters Degree holder and intelligent professional-to-be. This young teacher lost it right on the spot and told Fritz, "Take this job and . . ." He then stopped himself and told Fritz that his resignation would be on his desk in the morning.

This young teacher, being a man of his word, did exactly that.

Unlike those of us that had been jaded by the likes of Fritz, he had not yet learned to veil his teaching in the role of a sneak teacher. But he was young; He would learn in another school district. He had made the deal, left, and had saved his license. Dr. Fritz had failed another teacher. That young teacher, well, he had to rebuild his life. He left teaching. Once again, the losers were —— the kids.

Fritz entered into this new school year with revenge in his heart. He would not let a teacher tattle to a superintendent and survive in his school. Whatever it took, he would do it. In his mind, I was toast.

Chapter 21

Drugs Inc.

Big Guy had been to the executive headquarters of Drugs Inc. I don't really know what the organization was called, and none of us ever will. All I know is that it was an organization that did its business tax-free and in the shadow of night. The quarterly reports had been good, and Big Guy could report a nice increase in sales over the last quarter. The new steroid products were taking off as the athletic market was beginning to blossom. Ecstasy was moving nicely, since he had picked up some new junkies with connections to a group of kids with a desire to rave.

The con he had worked on two of his salesmen was working. He had told ZJ and LD, "You will have to make up the loss with interest paid on the lost dollar total." The alternative was that he would have the two of them eliminated, and for good.

He was bragging to his boss about the fact that he owned the two of them. "Those two are my slaves," he would joke. "I own those two, little jerks, boss, I own their asses."

ZJ, who had really turned on to drugs, was not too bothered by the threat; he was stoned most the time. Anyway, he could just get high anytime the thought crossed his mind that he owed $23,000, plus interest of 20% per annum.

LD was another story. He was, of the two of them, far more paranoid; drugs exacerbated this situation. The way out for him was to clear the debt. He worked hard to do this. He pushed ZJ to do more and riskier deals, the kind of deals that would eventually lead to a mistake. He was really paranoid about getting ripped off at gunpoint, like they had been at the hockey arena. He was paranoid about everything, and anything would send him into a rage. Afterward, he would become sullen.

Much to his dismay, he had flashbacks to that evening all the time. Sober or drugged, he would flash back. The hooded, gloved kid stealing the money and the car and shooting ZJ. It was about the most cold-blooded thing he had ever witnessed. The more dope he used, the worse it got; even booze didn't help. He was totally without help. No one was around that he could trust, except ZJ, and ZJ was stoned all the time.

The worse it got for LD, the better it got for Big Guy. The worse it got, the better the deals. LD was intent on paying off the debt, but it was growing so fast that it was like a dog chasing its own tail. The faster he went, the farther behind they got. Big Guy loved every minute of it. As a trained drug rehabilitation professional, he knew where it was headed, and he could care less.

The organization loved Big Guy; he had been sober for fifteen years and was the best producer they'd ever had. He wasn't a threat to the organization, as he was there for the money, not for the drugs. He was a cynic, and he was clean and sober. He was trusted to the extent that the organization was not in danger.

He had not committed a felony in many years and was not sought by the police. He was on his way up and he knew it. This allowed him access to the organization that others could not get. Most of the other pushers had a habit. Most of the pushers were like ZJ but had graduated to the next level of distribution.

The problem with most people in the business was that they, too, were hooked. Drug slaves are unreliable and untrustworthy. They were not good employees under any condition. They will also die of the disease that they have been introduced to. This is not conducive to long term relationships. The retraining of new drug reps is a big part of the business, and Big Guy was good at it.

The organization was reputed to have connections to South America. The top brass didn't live in this country and operated with impunity. The money was laundered internationally through Caribbean banks. The operation was a well-oiled machine that operated in the shadows of the world.

As Tipp O'Neil, the famous Speaker of The House once said, "All politics are local." So it is in the drug trade. Without the local Big Guy, the business fails to run. Without the ZJs and LDs of the world, the Big Guys fail. The business is nothing without access to the disease that feeds it. This is all done locally, and it's done in every neighborhood in America.

We are so easily convinced that the G-men of the DEA can stop the drugs at our border. According to Washington, we will win the "War on Drugs." But we have had twenty years of a War on Drugs, and profits for drug cartels do nothing but get larger and better every year. We tell our kids, "Just say no," and drug professionals laugh all the way to the bank.

We create programs like DARE. The drug professionals thank us for advertising their products. DARE hasn't worked. The War on Drugs hasn't worked, and anyone who tells you it has is probably working for Drugs Inc.

We are a very duplicitous nation when it comes to the disease of addiction.

We can't seem to get it. This is an epidemic, not a crime problem. We just don't get it. We send our children into the infected population of users that gather in our overcrowded high schools. We then wonder why they catch the disease. As the kids would say, "DUH."

I really believe that Drugs Inc. politically lobbies for the War on Drugs. They can treat the disease with their drugs, and that perpetuates the sickness. Drugs Inc. reaps the benefits of maintaining the status quo when customers are addicted for life. They don't have to advertise. They don't have to glamorize. They don't have to do anything to combat the DEA's war on drugs. They've won it before it even begins.

The disease has a pathology that is so obvious to the suppliers of illegal drugs that they realize the customer will seek them out at all costs. Even when threatened with jail, bodily harm, or even death, the junkies are so strong willed that they will do the work of finding drugs.

This takes the risk out of the equation for Drugs Inc. The organization has a productivity that is the envy of legitimate businesses. The customer does all the work and takes all the risk. The organization is like a machine that prints money.

Those who operate in this drug world include terrorists, revolutionaries, and the just plain greedy. The thugs that operate this business have no need for civility or humanity. Human life becomes a commodity to be bought and sold.

It is a perfect market without regulation and the added value of illegality. Illegal drugs are more expensive, because the risk of getting jail time adds value to the product. The nature of the disease of addiction creates customers for life. We have no cure for the disease. The best we can hope for is remission. This is a plague, not a crime.

All Big Guy wanted was a few salesmen like ZJ and LD, ten years in the business, and then off to the Caribbean to enjoy his new status. *I won't be Big Guy anymore; I'll be Rich Guy.*

Chapter 22

Pyrrhic Victory

For LD, the world just kept getting darker and darker. At times, in his sober moments, he thought about going to his parents and asking for help. After one notable yelling contest with Big Guy over money and compensation, he came home and tried to approach his dad. But, unknown to LD was the fact that his dad was a drunk, a functioning drunk, but a drunk, nonetheless. As LD approached him, he could see that his dad was drinking, which was not an unusual thing. LD knew that there were good days and bad days; there were sober days, drunken days, drunken sober days, and sober drunk days. He also knew that he couldn't count on his dad for anything; his dad was unpredictable.

LD had learned to cope with his dad's ways, and timing was everything. LD had a part-time dad. His moods would swing in wild fluctuations, from enormous generosity to deep depression with what seemed like total randomness. The good days were absolutely wonderful, although those days had seemed to disappear, as of late.

More and more, his dad would get into fights with his wife over nothing, and he was always barking ridiculous orders at LD. Once he had told LD, "If you don't come home with a straight-A report card, I'll kick you out of the house." LD, who was a C student, was without options, as it wouldn't happen no matter what his dad demanded. All of this is hard for a fifteen-year-old to understand. It's hard for anyone to understand.

LD carefully calculated his approach to his dad and cautiously addressed him.

"Dad." LD was careful to get his attention.

"What do you want?" LD listened closely for the hints as to his dad's state of mind. Convinced that the problem wouldn't wait and feeling pressured, he went forward with the conversation even when he wouldn't have normally done that. He was desperate for help.

"I got a problem," LD was being very sincere.

"We all got problems, kid," his dad was drunk and LD knew it.

The room went silent for what seemed to LD to be an eternity. Then, his dad revealed just how drunk he was with an attempt at some words, but "Ua ua wasifryed" was all that came out. The words were unrecognizable due to the slurring of his speech. For LD, this was like falling off the edge. "Kid, I got problems; you got problems; we all got problems. So what?" his dad was drunk but managed to get this point across.

This wasn't the time, and LD knew it. LD was not going to open up at all. Certainly not to a drunk that couldn't even show up for school functions going all the way back to grade school. His mother was not going to be any help, either; she had never been anyone but the person to call his father's work and tell them he was sick when he was too drunk, or too hung over, to go to work. She had tried in the beginning of the marriage, but was so lacking in her own self-esteem that she just did what she was told and was thankful that she had a roof over her head.

LD just went to his room, popped some pills, and turned the music up.

ZJ picked LD up in his recovered "Car-jacked" car the next morning. He still didn't have a driver's license. This morning was the same as any other school day. LD, in a hung-over haze, got in the car and said, "Look, ZJ, we have to clear this debt to Big Guy. So I'll tell you what we'll do!"

ZJ, taking another hit of coke off a piece of stainless steel that he kept in the ashtray of his car, said, in as cool a manner as possible, "What?"

"Look, 'E' is a big deal with the rave groups. Remember the day we got ripped off. One of our stops was to a customer of Big Guy's that was buying a big batch of 'E'. He was worth about $5,000 that night. Let's get in touch with that guy and set up a big buy. We'll offer a cheap price, a real deal if he takes five grand worth or better. Then, we'll rip him. Once we get the green, we pull a gun if we have to and Zero Junk him. Look, they're not hooked like the others; they won't be our customers in the future. They'll get their kicks and then move on to college and the good life. Let's rip them off."

LD's real point was, "Then, we can pay off most of our debt to Big Guy and get him off our backs. We've paid back a lot, but if we give him five grand in one hit, he'll have to back off," LD wasn't letting his desperation show.

ZJ really didn't care if Big Guy owned them, as long as he got his dope. In fact, the only reason he would go along with this rip-off was that as soon as they had the money, he would skim some off the top. He needed to party with some bad girls, anyway. Always thinking, he knew he would also further his image by pulling off a big rip.

"Go for it; set it up." ZJ was in.

Two nights later, LD and ZJ met a suburban preppy with five big ones in a paper bag looking to score big on the Ecstasy that the two had promised. He would be a hero to the ravers that he hung with. He had stolen the five grand from his dad. What was he thinking, that his dad wouldn't miss that kind of money? He was sure that he could get the "E" and sell it fast enough to replace the five grand. His dad would never know it was gone. But the money wasn't even gone five minutes and his dad was on to the problem. Preppy didn't know that yet, but he would find out — — that, I promise you.

The deal was going smoothly. They had met in the Diamond Ballpark parking lot. The preppy got out of his dad's SUV with the money in hand. Big mistake, 'cause ZJ got out of the car LD was driving. ZJ went to the trunk, opened it, took out a bag that looked like the ones that Big Guy used, and started walking toward the SUV. The preppy was naïve, but not stupid. He'd done a few deals with Big Guy and expected to get his dope, pay, and go. He had seen these two before, so he wasn't afraid.

As ZJ got closer to the preppy, the bags were visible even in the bad light. The preppy noticed that the bags had no preprinted label on them as he had become accustomed to. ZJ immediately knew that something was wrong, as the preppy backed away toward the SUV.

The whole thing was about to go bad. ZJ pulled his Glock, 9mm automatic from the back waistband of his pants. The preppy knew that he was in trouble. He handed ZJ the money, put his hands in the air, and then slowly got into his SUV and left, alive.

"Nailed him, huh, LD. Ripped him good, huh, dawg?"

"We sure did get him, ZJ, just one more naked

preppie. We stripped him of his money, and when a preppie don't have money, he's naked, ay, ZJ?"

The two got into ZJ's car and started driving, laughing, knee slapping, belly laughing, and laughing to excess. The adrenalin was running and the cocaine was accelerating the rush of adrenalin. The two believed that they had gotten away with this crime. ZJ reached into the bag and got out a handful of twenties, stuffed them in his pocket, looked at LD, and asked, "My commission, right?"

LD was disappointed, but he never said a word. LD knew, at that very moment, that his friend had taken his pleasures without regard to LD's welfare. Worse, for that matter, he didn't even offer the courtesy of a conversation. It looked like even ZJ was not going to listen to LD. LD was hurting big time, but ZJ was numb and without a clue.

Chapter 23

Who Let the Dogs Out?

Dr. Fritz got Nancy on the phone as soon as he arrived in the morning.

"Get ZJ in your office, first thing this morning," he demanded.

Nancy was curious, and asked, "What do you want me to do?"

"Tell him that we know he's been involved in a drug deal," Fritz sounded excited.

"Do we really know that he's been involved in a drug deal?"

"Yes."

"How do we know?" Nancy needed some facts to go on if she was going to face ZJ.

"Just believe me, we know." Fritz had something, but he was going to withhold it for the time being. He trusted no one, not even his closest allies.

"Tell him that it was the sale of Ecstasy." Nancy knew she had enough to get the conversation started.

"Do you have the goods on him?" Nancy inquired?

"Yes." No question about it, Fritz had him.

What Fritz wasn't telling her was that the preppy from the night before was the son of a friend of his from church that had called Fritz after he'd confronted his son about the missing five thousand dollars. The son had broken down and related the whole story to his dad.

He, in turn, knowing that the perpetrator was one of Dr. Fritz's students, had called Fritz. He'd told him the story in hopes of getting a solution without involving the police. Fritz had told him that he would see what he could do. Fritz figured that he could get a double bang out of this situation. One, he could force ZJ to get something on P, and then he could squeeze ZJ for the money after he got what he wanted.

"What?" was ZJ's reaction as he arrived in Nancy's office?

"Look, we have it on good authority that you were involved in a drug deal last night. E was sold, and you sold it," Nancy was fishing.

"What?" ZJ was surprised by the level of detail, but without LD there, he would have to figure out this one on his own, which was not something he did well.

She came right back at him, "You betcha we got you." She knew the dance steps as well as he did, both of them being veterans of the trip to the office waltz. She knew, however, that all she had to do was rough him up emotionally. Fritz would do the real dirty work on this one. No standoff today; this was the real deal, and she would be in on the kill. This was the part of the dance she was really going to enjoy. ZJ and all that were like him were seldom nailed outright. She knew that they had him. She knew who was taking who home from the dance.

"Nancy, get him going, I don't care what it takes. Lie, cajole, call him a jerk or an idiot; just get him."

She remembered the conversation from that morning and Fritz telling her to get him on the defensive. Wear him down a bit, and then call Dr. Fritz in. His order to get ZJ mad was not going to be easy because he knew the script, so she was going to try something new, "ZJ, your deal was found out last night, and we think that we'll get the police to go after your brother." Nancy began probing, remembering the last time he had been in her office. The conversation about his brother had been repeated last time he was in trouble.

It was working. ZJ became uncomfortable and there was some anger, as Nancy drove the point home, "ZJ, your brother is an adult, and if we can connect him with this crime, he goes to jail for quite some time."

ZJ was pissed now, and she could tell that it was just about time to bring in Fritz. She abruptly got up and said "ZJ, just sit here. I'll be right back."

The silence was horrible. He was left alone in Nancy's office.

In comes Fritz a half-hour later, "ZJ, you're in real trouble. Now just be quiet and listen carefully to what I have to say. I'm going to start bringing in kids and questioning them about drug deals that we know you were involved in. Then, I'm going to drop the hammer on you. That's right, ZJ, the worst assholes I can think of are going to be told that you are the source of the information that lead us to them. I'm going to tell them that you were involved in a deal gone bad. I will tell them that to save your own skin, you were telling all, naming names, and giving details. Then I'm going to expel them and turn them over to the police. I will see to it that they are in trouble *extraordinaire*. Every last one of them is going to know that you, LD, and your brother are turning states evidence to save your own skins."

"What the hell you saying? You know that my brother didn't have anything to do with any of this. He's gone and graduated from here, he has nothing to do with you or your stinking school." ZJ had lost it.

Fritz knew he had won this round, "Sure, you're right, but truth doesn't matter, punk, just appearances.

I don't expect you to understand what I can and cannot do; it doesn't matter to you. What should matter is that you, your brother, and LD will be marked on the street as narcs, little birdies that are singing to the police. We can get that done *and* get your brother on some bogus crap that will violate his court agreement in the hit and run case. He'll go to jail for a very long time."

ZJ's body did not like his mind at this moment. His mind was raw and hurting from the lack of drugs. The cravings for a fix were setting in. The detoxification of his body paled in contrast to the detoxification of his soul. The whole thing was most painful as he sobered up. After all, he was still a kid, and no matter how jaded he was, he was still just a kid.

Just as quickly as Fritz had put on the hard guy act, he now changed his tone and body posture to a softer position, "Look, ZJ, I can help you to... you know? But you need to help me. I can be your friend, or your enemy. All you have to do is help me. Life will return to normal; you can go on running your game, and all will be as it was."

"What?" ZJ was right in style.

"I need you to get a teacher for me," Fritz said softly.

"What?" ZJ was surprised at the request.

"I need you to get P. Maybe you can get LD to help." Fritz made it sound like an everyday occurrence.

"How?" ZJ was truly interested.

"I don't care; you figure it out and don't tell me. Just bring me the tale with enough facts that I can make it look good," Fritz was delegating the task.

"What?" ZJ truly didn't understand what Fritz was trying to do, but he did understand that he had a free shot at a teacher, and one he didn't care for, anyway. It was open season and an authority figure was the game, with no consequences.

"ZJ, you already took a run at him. This is your get-out-of-jail-free card. Try a little harder. Just remember to piss him off and then get to Nancy's office. Better yet, if you can get P to call the hall monitors, it will look better for me. Nancy will help you write a statement, so do whatever she says, write what she tells you, and absolutely nothing will happen to you or LD."

"And if I tell you to get fucked, then what?" Always testing, ZJ was in form.

"Then the dogs get let out and they bite your ass," Fritz was stern and direct.

"Okay, okay, give me a day or two." ZJ knew what he was going to do with the information he'd just heard.

Right after school, ZJ, LD, and the news showed up at Big Guy's apartment. They were sure this info was worth some free coke. Who could guess what Big Guy would do with the information? Both knew that it had value to him. Plus, they were delivering about four grand to pay on the debt. LD was starting to feel like he could see the end of this debt. He was feeling like the nightmare might end.

As soon as Big Guy had heard the first part, he said, "Stop right there, 'cause I got something for you guys." He went to the freezer compartment of his refrigerator and got out a bag of white powder. He handed a razorblade to them from the kitchen drawer and then laid out four lines on the glass coffee table. This was twice what he would have normally paid. He said to them with a big smile and a laugh, "Party, boys, party."

The two took out MacDonalds straws that had been shortened, and the four lines of snow disappeared.

"Now, finish the story," Big Guy encouraged them.

When they were finished with the tale, Big Guy had a really wide smile. He then took out the balance of the bag from the freezer and handed it to LD, "Thanks for the low down, Low Down." He had never done that before, called LD "Low Down." LD was thinking, *With the large payment and the good information we brought, the worst is over and we'll once again enjoy the status that me and ZJ had in middle school.*

LD handed Big Guy four thousand dollars. "Take it off our debt," LD demanded. Big Guy took the money, looked a bit puzzled, and said, "Done deal."

Chapter 24

Gameboy

ZJ and LD walked into my room with a Gameboy. We had not started class yet, so a Gameboy meant nothing to me. A Gameboy is an electronic hand held game.

I walked around the classroom, past the new tables that I had arranged to be used as computer workstations. As hall-passing time neared its end, I was less and less enthusiastic about the electronic game. The Gameboy was a simple toy like you would see at a retail store, about six inches in length. As problems in the room go, this wasn't a big one; it wasn't even a challenge. I would simply take the toy. Sometimes, I could get a chuckle by being a bit dumb about taking it.

I didn't know it yet, but LD was taking the lead on this one, "Hey, P-Daddy, what's up?" He was taunting me, and he was an expert at it. LD had lots of experience at this game, and I was just one more teacher to get to. *When he doesn't want to sleep, socialize, or sell drugs, a trip to the office must be quite entertaining,* I thought. *Working a teacher is great fun, and it's great advertising because it draws attention to the offender. This may just be advertising,* I was saying to myself.

"What do you want, LD?" I locked eyes with him and it didn't feel good at all; something was way too serious, this time.

"P-Daddy, you suck," he taunted me.

Not to be outdone, I fired back, "Well, that explains the noise in the back of the room. It must be the vacuum you created by being here, and vacuums make a sucking sound." I knew this was close to the line of good taste, but I had not stepped over it, yet.

"Hey, that's funny, P," his tone was as sarcastic as could be.

"Well, if you would like to put that Gameboy on my desk, I'll give it back at the end of class," I thought it was worth a try.

"Why don't you take it away?" How predictable LD was.

"If I come back there, I will," I stated this in my big teacher voice that left nothing to guesswork. He knew what I wanted.

This whole thing had turned deadly serious, and I did not like its direction. It was not time to call for help, but it was getting close. I knew at this point that the die had been cast and there was no turning back for any of us. It was going to play out and end badly. I had no idea how badly, at the time. Even if I had, it was one of those situations that leaves no options.

I remember thinking that all mankind must have certain scripts that when played out have bad endings. This situation leaves no room for creativity; not even humor was going to get me out of the game. I knew that the next lines of the script were not going to be a good thing.

"You suck, P. All these idiots sit here and worship you, and you just suck them in with your bullshit." The Gameboy was bouncing from hand to hand. LD was baiting me. It was in his attitude and his body language.

Finally, it was my turn to say the famous, ZJ quote, and as closely as I could mimic ZJ, while shrugging my shoulders and looking as goofy as I could, I asked, "What?"

"Yeah, you got it, asshole," that was two "Assholes" in the same hour —— LD was getting to me. "Most of these sons of bitches will end up being drunks and stoners. They'll never amount to anything. The school tells them they're no good from the day they arrive. Some bullshit authority is always right, and these kids are, and always will be, wrong. It was rigged from the beginning; these jerks don't stand a chance. They aren't bright enough to understand it."

LD was on a roll. Somehow, he had taken off in a direction I don't think even he had intended to go, but there he was. The anger was just spilling out. He then changed his focus from me to the class and went on.

"Yeah, you think they don't rig everything here? Well, they do. Dr. Fritz and his dudes decide who'll win and who won't. They select the chosen few in grade school. You stoners don't have a chance," LD was back to addressing me.

"These stoners take tests that they can't pass or even understand. They were doomed from the start. They were never taught to take tests, much less pass them. They were never given the chance to learn in ways that they could understand. They were just passed along so Fritz could get the money for them from the state.

Worse yet, be black or Asian, or, want a real laugh, be Mexican and try and get this place to care. There isn't a single black, red, or sand-colored teacher in this place. Not even the janitorial staff has a black," LD was cooking.

LD had a captive audience, and the anger was driving everything, now. He went on, "You!" He was pointing a finger at me, and he couldn't stay still, "You're the worst of all, because you've sold out to the bastards, and you're just a narc for them. You tell these kids, work hard, learn a skill, and you'll live happily, ever after. What a fucking fairytale!" LD was letting it all come out, all the anger, all the unfairness.

ZJ, sensing that the class was paying attention to LD, thought he saw an opening. He jumped in with both feet. "You think you're so goddamned funny, P. Well, you aren't; you're just a prison guard at this penitentiary for kids. That's right." He was looking right at me, "You think I'm so stupid. Well, if I'm so stupid, why can't you take a stupid game away from me?" he asked, as he grabbed the Gameboy from LD.

The class was out of their seats, now. They sensed the anger, and didn't want to be in the way when ZJ and LD started throwing punches.

It was my turn in this age-old contest. A challenge had been laid down by ZJ. *Take the Gameboy,* I thought, *Just take it and hold it in front of his face, like a statement of defiance.* I got up from my seat and started for him with a deliberate walk and that teacher look, stern and resolved.

I was mad as I approached, and getting madder. I had lost all control in my mind, though not just yet in the physical world. Then, a flashback, but nothing I could put my finger on. It was just a feeling at first. It's amazing how fast the mind works. Then it came to me, the look on Canna's face just before he kicked me. It was vivid, in color, and as I saw that anger in myself, I began to mellow. All this in the distance it took to walk from my desk to the young man. He was running a game, and he was running.

Then there was this old man remembering his worst day ever. Then, it hit me. I knew exactly what I was going to do. I would do nothing. You got it, nothing. That was what I was going to do. If I got hit, or if I got pushed, all real possibilities at the time, I was not going to do a thing. By the time I reached ZJ, I was at peace with myself, because I had reached a decision. I was simply a teacher, asking for a toy in a calm and cool way, and that was all.

"Please, give me the game," I said softly, with a certain grace that even I did not know I possessed.

"Come and get it, jerk!" ZJ was giving me the come on.

"Please, give me the Gameboy," I said, still using a soft tone.

"You think that because you order me around, I'll just do what you ask. I don't do nothin' I don't want to do, nothin'. I do the girls. I do to the junkies. I do to everyone who gets in my way. Hell, I'll do you, too."

He was taunting me, begging me to lose my composure, wanting me to take a swing, lip off, get down on him, and lose it.

"Please, give me the Gameboy," I went softer now, and then softer yet. I was falling into a defined cadence, "Please, give me the Gameboy," again, and again, and again, "Please, give me the Gameboy."

We were in a standoff, waiting for someone to blink. I really believed that I had defused the situation and that violence was not imminent. Finally, the blink; ZJ threw the Gameboy behind him on the floor. It took a funny bounce, like it had a spin on it, and it made a noise that all the students recognized as the ultimate win in the game. It was really a humorous moment.

Mother Nature and the laws of physics had stepped in to take the final edge off. No matter how serious ZJ tried to look, the path of the Gameboy and the music of the big win was just too funny for this group of kids to hold in their laughter. First snickers, then a giggle, and then all out laughing. Worse yet, ZJ was beginning to look really dumb, and he knew it.

The gods had spoken, and the cards had gone against him.

Chapter 25

The Big Lie

Fritz was standing behind his big, oak desk with the oak veranda behind him. This is the same class of furniture that one might find in a Fortune 500 CEO's office. He was mad, and he was yelling as loud as he could at ZJ, "What the hell?"

"Look, I tried everything, Dr. Fr—" Fritz wouldn't allow him to even finish a sentence, but ZJ was actually trying to calm him down, which was unusual behavior for ZJ.

"ZJ, you didn't so much as get him to even raise his voice!" Fritz yelled again. ZJ had made a deal and it hadn't worked. No one could just keep taking shots without it becoming obvious that something was out of place. Fritz was really angry that this had not yielded results.

"We'll get him, Dr. Fritz, next time," ZJ was trying to reassure him.

"Look, ZJ, you and LD are going to write statements that I give you. Just write them in your own handwriting. Nancy will coach you; don't skip a word she tells you, got it?"

Fritz was committing fraud, and he was instructing ZJ as to how he would become complicit in the crime.

"What?" ZJ looked puzzled.

"Just do as you're told." Fritz was still mad, and

ZJ was still very aware of the threats that had been made concerning his brother's and his own wellbeing.

Walking down the narrow hall to Nancy's office, ZJ picked up LD on the way. LD had been sitting in one of the bad boy's chairs in the hall.

Nancy handed them each a typed statement that was created by her, "Okay, here's the statement I want you to write. Got it? Copy this, word for word." The statement had been carefully crafted to achieve a specific objective.

The statement read, "I walked into class with a Gameboy. P came over to me and said, 'Give me that Gameboy.' I asked, 'Why?' P pulled a knife from his pocket, whipped it open, and said he was going to open the battery door on the back of the Gameboy. The knife threatened me because I felt it was a terrorist threat. I moved away, so he put the knife back into his pocket and asked me for the Gameboy again, and I said, 'Only if you give it back at the end of the hour.' I turned it over to him and got it back at the end of the hour."

ZJ wrote out the statement.

He had just perjured himself on a Northwest High incident report. He had dated it and signed it according to Nancy's instructions. LD's statement was just a little bit different, but it said the same thing. He also dated it and signed it. He, too, had perjured himself.

"We finally have the SOB," Nancy was talking to herself, rehearsing the points that she would make when she went into Fritz's office.

With statements in hand, Nancy trekked down the hall after sending the two liars back to their class. She arrived, beaming, in Fritz's office. She announced, "We have him." Fritz smiled and looked the statements over. He stated that he would call the two boys' parents and get the ball rolling on the investigation. The charges would be better received by the board of education if the parents initiated the proceedings. That would be more credible than if he started the investigation himself.

Nancy looked at him with a smile that would make a devil shiver. She bragged and stated the obvious, "We've got him."

Dr. Fritz looked at the statements, looked at Nancy, and said, "The least that the son-of-a bitch could have done was swear, or yell, or something. He didn't even yell at the other kids; he didn't do anything at all. What's up with him, doesn't he get angry? Well, it doesn't matter; we've got enough with these two statements to open a criminal investigation." He felt that he had me now.

"Nancy, go to our good teachers and tell them that P is under a criminal investigation on a weapons charge. Lay on the words 'Weapons' and 'Criminal Investigation' as much as possible. Let the word spread on the school grapevine. Spread the gossip as fast as you can. You know which teachers to get this to. Our window of opportunity is very small, as the kids will not lie about what happened in the room. We'll have to get these reports to the police as quickly as possible." Fritz was pleased, and it showed in his expression.

There was a moment of silence in the room as the gravity of what the two were planning set in. Then Fritz chimed in, "I was hoping we could get an arrest during class hours with handcuffs and a police escort out of the building. We'd better be careful here; this might not work, so I want only rumors for now. Maybe P will make a mistake."

He went on to instruct her, "Get him down to your office. Send Grace, the hall monitor, to get him. Tell her to be as rude and disruptive to his class as possible.

That will start the rumor with the kids who weren't in the class that the incident took place. Have her direct him to your office. He will not come to my office without a union rep." Fritz seemed to resent my caution.

"Once he's in your office, start in on him, demanding to see the contents of his pockets. He has a jackknife, and I know he has it on him. I've seen him use it in his room to strip wire. As soon as you have the knife on the table, ring me. Don't use my name, and I'll come right over."

Fritz had to think for a moment, and then said, "Nancy, he will not be expecting this. Once he's in your office, we will pressure him, two on one. You and I will gang up on him. He'll blow up; they all do, eventually."

He went through his mental checklist and said, "Nancy, one last thing, call the cops and get them over here. If we get lucky, he might do something stupid. Don't let up on him. Don't let him talk; just keep making accusations. Accuse, accuse, accuse, and let him read the statements. Get him copies to read. Use statements to lead him along. Now, get to work." Fritz was excited.

Nancy called the police, got copies of the reports, and sent Grace to get me.

Grace walked into my room with a mission and a swagger. She yelled at me from across the room, "Nancy's office, right now! You hear me, P? Right now! This is an emergency. You're to go, right now! I'll stay here!"

My first thought was that one of my children or my wife had been hurt. I turned and was about to walk out of the door, when Blake, a student aid, lobbed a VHS tape to me. I caught the tape as I walked out the door.

"P, this might help. It's the ZJ and LD debacle from this morning," I will always wonder if Blake knew what was happening better than I.

This tape was of the incident that had occurred that morning between me and two junkies. Blake was an amateur video guy. He knew more than I ever gave him credit for. He had gotten wind that something was going to happen to me. He had acted on his own and had turned on the surveillance system, the one that he'd installed earlier in the week. It had captured the whole thing when ZJ and LD had flown off the handle. He'd filmed everything. Bless that child's heart.

I caught the tape, not for a moment thinking to put the tape down. I was sure that the next thing I was about to hear was that I had a real tragedy on my hands. I was sure that one of my loved ones was in some kind of trouble, and Grace did nothing to dispel that idea.

I arrived at Nancy's office to be met by her and Officer Strand of the North St. Paul police.

I just knew, the minute I walked into her office, that I would hear about the death of my daughter or my wife. I was especially sure of this when I saw the police officer. I was terrified and asked God for His mercy.

Nancy looked at me and said, "Empty your pockets on the desk, right now."

My reaction was relief, and it wasn't exactly the reaction she was expecting, as I asked, "What the heck is this about?" I was thanking God that I wasn't hearing about some horrible accident.

Nancy handed me two written reports that were dated for today and sneeringly said, "Read these and weep, and empty your pockets on the desk! Now!" She was yelling at me in a tone that was not very becoming.

I didn't empty my pockets, but I did read the reports. I didn't say a word.

Then, I became aware that the cop was there to arrest me. I issued this warning to both of them, "If either one of you pursue this, big trouble will follow; I can guarantee it." I was calm, but my voice held resolve. I meant it and they were both a bit surprised. I also demanded union representation.

"Yeah, yeah, they all say that stuff when confronted with Officer Strand," Nancy was trying to provoke me. She looked the officer right in the eye and demanded, "I want him arrested for weapons possession and brandishing a weapon on school grounds," Nancy was excited, big time. She knew, or thought she knew, that I had made a threat that I couldn't back up. She thought she had me, and she was moving in for the kill.

"I will say this one more time, you are both in trouble if you do anything," I was determined and assertive, not yelling, just stern.

Strand, the cop, looked at Nancy and asked, "Nancy, what's he talking about? He means business, and I don't know you well enough to take a risk with this. What's going on here, and what have you gotten me into?"

Then he turned to me and said, "Look, Mr. P, we have two corroborating statements of an incident. Do you think that these two are lying?" Strand was really getting suspicious now. The reports were very clear; yet here stood a teacher who was not one bit scared. In fact, here's a teacher making threats that guilty people don't make. He's not angry, he's not protesting too much, and he's not asking for a lawyer, so something ain't right.

The intuition of this street cop was telling. This was big trouble for him down the road. A younger cop might have just arrested me and would have been done with it, but this cop was smarter and more seasoned than that.

"P, I need you to clarify the reported incident. Did you or didn't you pull a knife?" Strand was at least asking questions.

"No, I didn't," I was adamant.

"Hold on a minute." Strand turned to the vice-principal, "Nancy, I get called down here because you tell me you have a teacher, dead to rights, on a weapons charge. You call for an arrest and then an investigation. How come I'm thinking that this may be a mistake?" Strand was looking Nancy right in the eyes.

"Just arrest him and you can straighten out the rest later," Nancy demanded. She had a feeling that she wasn't going to get what she wanted. She wanted me, "The perp," to walk through the school with handcuffs on and being escorted by a uniformed officer.

I looked Strand right in the eye and said, "If you know that you're involved in a fraud and proceed in any way, I'm sure that your life as a police officer will change." Now I was gaining ground, and I could feel the tide turning my way.

"The hell, you say?" Strand was getting concerned, but not backing away, "You threatening me?" He was getting hot.

"Yes, and I will sue and win," I delivered that line in as matter-of-fact a way as I knew how.

"What makes you so sure of yourself?" Strand wasn't taking any of this lightly, at this point.

"Just believe me; you don't have a chance. You can take my word as a professional, or you can start something you can't finish. You haven't done a thing here to investigate the charge............"

I never got to finish the sentence, as he interrupted me and said, "Hold it, no one has charged anyone with anything." He was backpedaling as fast as he could. I could tell that he realized he wasn't confronting some street scum or a drunk driver; he must have figured out that he was standing in a vice–principals' office and becoming tangled up in the middle of what was obviously a personnel or management problem and which had nothing to do with the breaking of any laws. Whatever the weapons charge, if there was one at all, he was getting out of this situation as quickly as he could. He didn't care how he did it, because the liability to him grew by the second. He could easily be charged with false arrest, and if I struggled, I would claim abuse of power and the charges would go on and on. He would lose his job and probably have to defend himself in court. All this was enough to give him pause. The probable loss of his pension wasn't worth this.

"Nancy, get Dr. Fritz in here, now," Strand demanded.

I jumped in at this point, knowing that a yelling contest was about to begin.

"Not without a union rep."

Strand knew why I wanted a union rep and he backed me up, "Get a union rep in here, also, Nancy."

What seemed like hours passed, as Nancy went and got Fritz who had been waiting for the call. He was really irritated that the scene had not developed the way he had expected. She also went and got Denny out of class.

I was pretty sure that I had defused the situation. I certainly hoped that I had.

Fritz walked into Nancy's office before Denny had arrived, and, sensing a window of opportunity, he demanded, "Officer, search this man immediately. I know that he carries a jackknife as described in the incident report."

I was thinking at the speed of light now, as I could clearly see who was behind all this, so I jumped in, "Yes, I do carry a jackknife, and I also have a shop teachers license that allows me to do just that, and until you have a court directive banning such use, I will continue to carry a jackknife," boy, was I cocky now.

Before I could get out another word, Denny arrived with an edict, "If we need an attorney here, I need to know right now, officer. If these are criminal charges, I need to get this man an attorney, right now." Denny didn't know what had happened, but he knew Fritz.

Strand looked a bit surprised at Denny's aggressiveness. He immediately made it clear that he had a reason to be there in as much as a weapons charge had been alleged.

"P, who is accusing you?" Denny inquired.

I jumped in so that Denny would know what was up, "ZJ and LD."

Strand didn't wait for Fritz at this point, because he now had faces that he could place with the Christian names he had read in the incident report. He hadn't recognized the formal, Christian names that LD and ZJ had used to sign the incident reports.

Officer Strand looked Fritz right in the eyes and asked, "Dr. Fritz, you called me down here because ZJ and LD told you some crap? You've got to be kidding me. We both know ZJ and LD to be two of the biggest junkies in town, and you call my ass down here to arrest a teacher based on the testimony of two dopers?"

Strand knew he'd been had. He was angry now, and not just a little angry, but the kind of angry that made one sure he was thinking, *You had better never go even one mile over the speed limit in this town, Fritz and Nancy.* He was really pissed off.

Fritz barked at him, "Strand, if I say so, you have

to open an investigation based on any student's written statement, and you know it."

"OK, if that's the way you want it." Then Strand turned to me, "P, why did you warn me not to pursue this when I first came in?" Strand was going to take control at this point, and he was curious as to why I had been so resolved.

I looked at Strand and once again launched into the "You'd better not" speech. I threatened him again with a lawsuit and anything else I could think of. Never once did I lose my cool. I just stated my case as factually as possible. I looked around the room to see if I had everyone's attention. Then, and only then, did I make it clear that I had the goods.

"I can prove in spades that none of what these two are saying is even remotely close to the truth, and I'm not kidding anymore," this caught all of them by surprise.

Strand was really irritated at this point, "Dr. Fritz, I don't know this teacher, at all, but I do know ZJ and LD."

Now his voice went up about an octave and he was getting red in the face as the anger came to the surface. "You are not being sincere with me, Dr. Fritz. This situation is becoming incredibly out of hand and is totally without any merit at all." Again, Officer Strand went at him, "You'd better tell me what you're after, because I don't think that screwing a teacher is on my agenda for today. What the hell is this all about, Fritz? And I want to know, right now."

Fritz started to say, "You have to—" when I interrupted him and looked to Officer Strand.

"Let me talk to Denny, alone, just for two minutes, Officer?" I requested.

"Okay, we'll leave." Strand was really pissed, and

everyone knew it.

As soon as they left, I looked at Denny and said, "Denny, I really don't know what's going on here, but believe me, those two jerks, LD and ZJ, are lying, and I can prove it."

"How?" Denny was really astonished.

I walked over to the VCR in Nancy's office and put in the tape. I then handed Denny a copy of the statements that the two had written. After I went over and closed the door to Nancy's office, I hit 'Play' on the remote. Denny was reading the statements and trying hard to see the tape.

The whole scene took about two minutes. I was front and center in the TV screen along with ZJ and LD. The tape was dated and timed in the corner of the screen. During the whole incident, my hands were visible and there was no knife.

Denny didn't even take the time to speak with me; he simply went to the door, opened it, and said, "Officer, please come in here. You two, stay out there," he was pointing at Fritz and Nancy.

As Strand walked into the office, he said, "This had better be good."

"Oh, it is," Denny said, and he was laughing. He closed the door, looked at me, and winked. He then pushed 'Play' on the VCR.

Chapter 26

Compromise, I Think?

Denny was standing squarely in front of Fritz's big oak desk, directly across from the seated Fritz. Fritz was starched stiff, his shirt, his pants, and everything was perfect, including his silver gray hair. He was the perfect image of a CEO from a Fortune 500 company. He had an exclusive address in North Oaks, the gated community of St. Paul, the north end home of the rich. He belonged to the North Oaks Country Club. He saw himself as the executive that had not been discovered by the big boys, whoever they were. What a swagger for a guy making $100,000 a year and living in the world of Visa cards and second mortgages in the big house in a gated community of the really rich. He was a ten-cent millionaire, living on cheap beer and talking the talk with no ability to walk the walk. He just kept piling up more debt. The American Dream, right?

Fritz, with no conscious or moral fiber, leaned back in his chair and stated to Denny, in no uncertain terms, "Denny, I don't care what the tape shows; I'm not about to punish those two boys."

Denny was totally frustrated at this point, yet he hadn't lost his composure. Fritz sensed his frustration and that Denny was close to the edge, so just like a wolf moving in for a kill, Fritz sensed the imminent loss of control on Denny's part. This was the moment that Fritz lived for, when he gained total control through his opponent's loss of control.

Denny went on, "The statements are false. These two children would have had P's livelihood terminated if you had not been stopped. But for the fact that the situation is visible in black and white on dated film, you would have fired him, at the least, and have had him arrested if you could. This gives you no room for half-truths, for out of context statements, or for guilt by association. These two boys are guilty, and we, the teachers union, want them punished."

Fritz was not moved at all, and he was all but distracted by the rhetoric that was coming from Denny. "All of that may be true, but it will take a lot of time and effort you don't have to even get this heard by anyone who would care. I have it covered at the district with the superintendent. I have all my bases covered." I might have thought of this as bravado in anyone else, but with Fritz, this was a statement of fact. "So, just drop it," he was done with Denny.

Fritz was silent for what seemed an eternity, and then he made eye contact with me.

I think it's important, at this point, to take a moment and explain how teacher contracts really work. Common thought is that teachers belong to this union that protects bad teachers and keeps administrators at arm's length from the teachers. Well, that's what people think.

The way it really works is, first off, it's hard for a school district to fire a teacher. The other side of that coin is that it's impossible for a teacher to change to a new school district. The biggest reason is the union rules that govern seniority. Once a teacher has been tenured, usually three years, they are locked into a contract that is dependent on the number of years the teacher has been in service in that district. If a teacher leaves a district for another assignment, they must start at the bottom of the pay scale. This means starting all over again. They have to be tenured in that new district just like they had been in the old. This puts a teacher at risk, as they become an employee at will during periods of non-tenure with very few, if any, contract rights. Once a teacher is tenured in a district, they rarely leave.

Remember, a district owns you and they like it that way. This prevents good teachers from bidding up the price of their services and it keeps other districts from raiding the staff of good schools. It is a protection for districts that hire in the early years of a teacher's career. School districts don't want that changed. What they do want is to have their cake and eat it, too, by having teachers locked into a district but still be able to fire a teacher at will. This way, districts could fire older teachers as they climbed the pay scale, replacing them with the younger teacher willing to work for lower wages.

Fritz began to speak with a renewed authority, as Denny was not sure how to approach this problem, "Look, P, you got lucky. I will not reprimand you in any form," as if he could, "so why don't you go back to class and do your job? I'll eventually get you. I'll build a file of small infractions, if necessary. I don't care how long it takes," he said this with determination.

"You're a glib and witty individual who opens himself up to all kinds of interpretations of your rhetoric, both in and out of the classroom. It will take me more time than I would like to spend, but I *will* get you. You can't leave the district without a severe reduction in pay and status."

"We both know that you're guilty of this weapons charge. Well, I missed you this time, but I won't the next time, as I'm still your boss, and I hold all the cards. You will say something to a teacher or a child that will get back to me. We will investigate and get you written up. We will eventually get you. You can't teach without saying things that can be taken out of context and used against you. In fact, the more honest you are with the kids, the more vulnerable you become. You'll say something I can claim is sexual, illegal, or immoral. You'd better believe that guys like you, who think they're so good, are the at most risk."

"So if you're going to keep your job, you're going to do little more than take attendance. If you don't believe me, think for a moment. Two junkies, I own them, and kids talk."

"Teachers are the worst. They're all thinking that by competing for my ear, they'll get something that they wouldn't otherwise receive. They're all their own worst enemies ever since Reagan and the enrollment decline of the eighties. We've been able to divide you teachers; make no mistake."

"I was here in the late seventies and early eighties, and I wouldn't have been tolerated, acting as I do. But times have changed. I have to work hard to get rid of you old assholes, but I get it done, and the boys in the front office love it."

"Don't think for one minute that you're going to pull any of that age discrimination crap on me, either, because you old guys don't win those lawsuits. The law is so lame that it might as well not exist. One last thing, and Denny will confirm this; turn in your colleagues and you get ahead; keep to yourself and you go first," Fritz was out of breath, but he had made his point.

All during the speech he had just given, his body language, his tone, and his eye contact were all saying, "Make my day; get pissed off at any one of the things that I just said. Lose your temper, and I have you." Worse yet, he wasn't even done yet; he was on a roll.

"Fear me; it's the answer to longevity here at old Northwest High. It's the way to run a good school, and the board agrees or they would fire me. Teachers do what I want or they leave. Most leave of their own accord, as, eventually, will you. Some, I pack their file until it takes them down, and some just blow up and give up."

"Just like I can't fire you, you can't fire me. This conversation is over. Both of you, leave now," Fritz was ordering us out.

We left, with our ears stinging from the truth that had just been laid out before us. Neither one of us spoke, but I thought that I might just take up drinking again.

I didn't take up drinking again.

Chapter 27

Game Plan

The days after that encounter were quite peaceful, for the most part. I went to my classroom, free of the need to hide meaning in coded language. I no longer felt the need to teach with body language and winks, and I no longer needed the sneak teaching methods that had helped me survive as a teacher up to this point. At least, not for the time being. I was out in the open. What I did just didn't seem to matter anymore; I was going to get in trouble no matter what I did.

In fact, the incident had a certain honesty to it. I knew my days were numbered, so I no longer cared what Fritz did or caught me doing. It freed my soul from the drudgery of conformity for the sake of my job. Now, I just wasn't afraid to teach. It was intoxicating, and despite the fact that I hadn't had a drink in thirty years, I was intoxicated with joy, great peace, and energy.

I would ask questions that I knew would force the kids to think. The discussions were great. We talked about dating; We talked about drugs and alcohol; We talked about everything young adults need to talk about. These kids had been starved for real conversation, and the debates were fantastic. That's what teaching is all about, the delivery of information in an active, open discussion, where you feel safe and can explore. We talked and talked and talked.

We didn't fail in our primary mission, either. We drew houses, lake cabins, car transmissions, rollerblades; you name it, we drew it, including the kitchen sink, literally, we drew the kitchen sink. The quality of our work soared, and it amazed me that these kids could draw detailed house plans, intricate cutaways of mechanical objects, and also discuss civil rights at the same time. They wanted to know how the real world worked, not the version a teacher that had just graduated from college was selling, and not the cloistered textbook tale that is taught in most mainstream high schools. They wanted the nitty-gritty about how things worked. I was really proud of their progress. ZJ and LD got bored and went to sleep on most days, or, they were noticeably absent.

I was going home every night feeling like I had made a difference. Now, I don't want to seem to paint too rosy a picture, because the work of learning still had to be done. The paperwork didn't go away, and the committee meetings were still there. All the kids weren't perfect. I still had the high jinx that all high school teachers put up with, including the mice that were kept in one of my computers.

To this day, I still don't believe the tale that was being told about the great mice farce. When those kids, now adults, return to tell me the tale, I always accuse them of "Whopperising," of outright lying. The tale gets better every year.

I will tell you this and I mean it; I was going home each night very proud of the progress, and I was tired but not beaten. I was always looking forward to the next day. I was fully alive.

My classroom was a vibrant and special place to be, even for the less than brilliant students. In fact, I learned that it was not the smart ones I helped the most, but those who had struggled through school. We all laughed, cried, and cared. I loved it.

I still had to deal with the rumor mill and the smear campaign that had been started by Fritz. Even though we had the film of LD and ZJ, there were those on the staff that still told everyone that I had brandished a weapon and should be arrested and fired. The kids laughed at the lies. Some of the teachers, in as hurtful a way as possible, would ask when I would be fired, but nothing happened to me. This was a humiliation that Fritz just couldn't take.

Dr. Fritz called ZJ and LD into his office for a conversation. Fritz informed them that they were going after P one more time, and this time, they were going to get it right, "You two aren't going to get the chance to screw this up. Got it?" Fritz was mad.

The two were amused, then cynical, and finally, they got in Fritz's face. They knew that they owned Fritz for the moment. They had entered into a fraud with him. Big Guy had explained, in junkie terms, the power they now had if they choose to use it. Big Guy had told them, "Don't use your ace in the hole until you need to get out of a drug bust or a jam." But they were feeling a mite powerful at the moment.

"We aren't doing your dirty work, any more," LD declared.

"Fuck it!" ZJ was being brave, as well as testing to see what Fritz would do. "You can't get the job done with written lies. You can't get the job done, period. You're one cold son-of-a bitch for asking us to do this, Fritz. You put us in a real tough spot; we did as you asked and you blew it."

"You two little punks are going to do as I say. You got it?" Fritz was trying to get their attention.

Slowly ZJ pulled a cell phone out of his pocket and dialed in Big Guy's number. You could tell that someone had answered at the other end because ZJ started to speak, "Look, don't ask me nothin' and just answer my questions."

Big Guy usually didn't hear from ZJ during school hours and had told him never to use his cell in school to call him as someone might take his number off the recent calls recall on the phone. But, the damage had been done, and ZJ had Big Guy's curiosity up.

"Look, LD and I are in Fritz's office, and it's like I told you before, he wants us to do some more dirty work for him," ZJ was taunting Fritz as much as letting Big Guy in on the action.

Big Guy was direct, "Find out exactly what he wants."

"I really don't care what he wants; he put us in a tough spot last time and he fucked it up," again with the baiting. ZJ was having a good time.

"All the more reason to get the scoop, then get over here and I'll tell you what to do." Big Guy wanted time to think.

Fritz knew he had a new partner, but he didn't seem to care. He was on a mission.

"Okay, Fritzy, tell us what the hell you want us to do," again, ZJ was testing new ground on which to display his irreverence for the unwanted partner he was working with. Fritz was in, and so was Big Guy, even though they did not know each other.

"I want to get P in a room with a girl, all by themselves," Fritz started to unfold the script he had envisioned.

"Ya hear that?" ZJ was yelling at the cell phone to Big Guy. He then placed the phone back to his ear.

"Look, ZJ," Big Guy directed, "tell him we'll take

care of him. Tell him you'll do as you're told, then get your ass over to my place right after school for instructions." Big Guy was the boss, and ZJ was going to do as he was told.

"Okay, Fritzy," ZJ agreed, "tell us what to do, or better yet, we'll tell you how to do it. Just tell us what you want to happen, and me and LD will get back to you," ZJ was attempting to take over.

Dr. Fritz had just made a Faustian deal, without realizing to what extent he would have to pay for the favor. Blank checks can be expensive.

Later that afternoon, the security buzzer went off in Big Guy's apartment, and then ZJ and LD were coming up the stairs. He left the apartment door open for them.

"I want you to get one of the ghetto girls that you're banging, a good ho that will do as she's told. Maybe you could use that Brenda girl, the one whose parents are drunks. She really likes you, ZJ. She'll do anything you ask. Offer her enough green to make it worth her while," Big Guy was laying out the plot.

"Hell, Big Guy, we owe you thirteen thousand dollars, plus interest! Now, how am I gonna pay her? She, sure as hell, ain't doin' nothin' without being paid. Christ, we'll never get out of debt. How the hell do we operate without some dead presidents?" ZJ was trying to bargain on the debt and get some operating capital.

"I'll pay her; you can tell her that. She knows who I am, and she'll play," Big Guy was sure of himself.

"Okay, but what are we going to do?" LD wanted to know, as he was about to work his own deal.

"I'll tell you when I'm ready. Now, what I want you to do is get an audio tape of Fritz telling you that you are going to 'Do' this teacher. Go to Radio Shack and get a small recorder. Don't let Fritz know your taping him. I want Fritz on tape saying shit we can use. Got it?" Big Guy was doing what all great criminals are famous for, getting the goods on someone and then extorting favors.

ZJ and LD did as they were told, but not before getting a couple of hundred from Big Guy, and, at LD's insistence, without it being added to their debt. He was bothered by the state of the debt and how slowly it was getting paid off. LD put up a fuss about the debt and told Big Guy that if this worked, the debt would be canceled, paid in full. *Big Guy agreed just a little too easy,* LD thought, but he wasn't going to argue when Big Guy had just agreed.

As ZJ and LD were on their way to the store, LD looked at ZJ with a truly puzzled look on his face. He started to speak cautiously to ZJ.

"ZJ, you ever think about getting clean?" LD was not kidding.

"Fuckin' right, just like you do. We all do," ZJ was sincere.

"Then, what's stopping you?" LD was onto an honest conversation, the first one he'd had with ZJ in a long time. It felt good; this was the old ZJ that had once cared about his friend.

"It's just like with your old man; he keeps trying but he never gets sober. Every time he says that he is going to quit, he goes straight for a week, two weeks, a month, then he's right back on the juice," ZJ was being frank.

"I think I can get clean," LD announced.

ZJ didn't like this subject. He had no intention of ever getting clean. He'd thought about it now and then, but he was still at the stage where it was a lot of fun to get wrecked and laid. He had money; he had girls, and best of all, he didn't have to face any of the consequences of his actions.

In an attempt to change the subject, he abruptly looked at LD and said, "You want to get some girls, or do you want to use your hand like those goody-two-shoes bastards we hate. The fastest way to get laid is to pay for it. You'll get all you ever wanted, whenever you want it. Those jocks and geeks, they get nothing. And you, you get it all the time, and as long as you use protection, you get it risk free. Think about it, man."

"Yeah, yeah, you're right, *maybe*," LD wasn't buying.

"Maybe nothing, asshole. You're just going to end up a drunk like your old man, anyway. At least this way, you get pussy," ZJ was selling hard.

"I have a feeling we're in bigger trouble than you think," LD was now doing a reality check that ZJ didn't want to hear.

"What?" ZJ trusted LD, and only LD. He had known LD all his life. They went all the way back to kindergarten. They were like brothers, and when LD gave a warning, ZJ listened. It had saved his life more than once.

"We're in deep with Big Guy, so we have no choice but to deal big time. Big Guy isn't going to let us pay off this debt. Why do you think he keeps heaping on charges and interest. He has people he answers to, and those assholes are cold, real cold, and you know it. We're trapped in this game, and if I have to be here, I'm going to be sober; you got it?" LD was searching for the will to do something about his addiction.

"Sure, sure you are. I'll believe it when I see it," ZJ was challenging him now.

The two bought what they needed at Radio Shack and then went to ZJ's garage, as ZJ's mom was never home.

She was working all the time and earning a minimum-wage income that was barely enough to maintain their middle-class lifestyle. However, if you add the profits from some illegal narcotics deals, you can get by.

As soon as they had the equipment working, they called Big Guy to get instructions. Big Guy told them get it done.

During my class the next day, the two asked if they could go down to the office, an unusual request from them. I called the office and Nancy told me to send them down. This struck me as unusual. I had requested through formal channels that the two be punished for their part in trying to get me fired, so I figured they might be trying to make a deal. I didn't know. I still thought that something might happen.

ZJ and LD were especially cool as they sat down in the chairs in front of Fritz's desk. LD had closed the door.

"Fritzy, tell us how you plan to get P in bed with some jail bait? Tell us in detail how you plan to get P in deep enough to get him fired?" ZJ took the lead.

"I don't need to get him to do anything except be in a room alone with one of those girls that is willing to accuse him of certain things. We need someone with a reputation who is willing to point a finger at him," Fritz had the plan scripted.

"Who in this school would do that to P-Daddy?" LD was curious as to what Fritz was really doing with whom.

"I've got students that owe me. They're in debt to me big time, and I own them," Fritz was bragging to these young junkies. How pathetic is that.

"Right, Fritz, sure you do. You don't even know your own school. There ain't nobody in this school who you can trust to do that. The other kids will pressure them into telling the truth. They all look up to P. Even if you do have someone that owes you that much, you're takin' a big risk. We can supply you with the right person, and we'll take care of it," ZJ wanted control.

"You two have screwed it up every time. I'm going to take care of this myself, and you'd better just do as you're told. Play the part just as I tell you," Fritz was not going to give up control.

The two were not about to take the blame for Fritz's lame attempts to get P, and ZJ was especially provoked. He took aim at Fritz and started testing. For a kid with nothing to lose, it means nothing to take a shot.

He didn't care anymore what Fritz thought. He had tested enough, at this point, to know that Fritz was going to take anything he was handed. Fritz was going to take it, regardless of how crude it might be. It was the attempted testing that was not answered that was revealing to a child's mind. ZJ was just a kid, but he had learned this trick.

"You doin' these chicks, or what? Why else would you be so sure you can get 'em to make a statement against P?" ZJ was testing new ground.

"I don't 'Do chicks,' you little asshole," Fritz was mad now.

ZJ had hit a nerve, and he knew it. More testing.

"So you ain't gettin' none at home?" Now, ZJ was bold and out of bounds.

"Shut up!" Fritz was yelling now.

"Spankin' the monkey, asshole?" ZJ had him going; Fritz was mad and out of control. The crude comment had hit pay dirt, and it was all on tape.

Fritz was really pissed now. He was not used to having street dirt questioning him in this way. He was really losing it when ambushed by this street punk. The dirty allegations were more than he could take, and ZJ, LD, and Big Guy were about to get what they wanted.

"You two are just a couple of street punks who will end up in prison or dead. P wants your asses for lying. I know that you're lying; you know you're lying, and I can hand P a libel suit that will cost your parents plenty," Fritz had just revealed the real Fritz.

The two burst into laughter. They were looking at each other and were so involved in the laughter that they were actually crying. They were totally out of control. Fritz had never seen such behavior. They both knew that they had him cold. It would never be used in a court of law. There was no law in Drugland. There were no civil proceedings in Drugland. There was just the world according to Big Guy, and the extraction of blackmail, extortion, and the selling of souls. The two intuitively knew that they had just won and now they could leave if they wanted. It was just too great a moment not to savor the victory.

Fritz didn't have a clue.

When the two finally started to control themselves, it was LD who first realized the irony of the situation.

"Heavy stuff, ZJ," he said with a wink in his voice. "Fritzy don't get nothin' at home, gets pissed off and tells us he's gonna get my drunk-ass dad sued. Wow, am I scared or what? He must not have read 'Brer Rabbit' when he was little, 'Oh, please don't fling me in dat brier-patch!' What a joke!" LD was toying with him and enjoying every moment.

Then, the two started mocking Fritz by saying in unison, "Oh, please don't fling me in dat brier-patch!"

Fritz didn't know it, but he was really fighting a Tar-Baby.

ZJ finally looked at Fritz and chuckled, "If you want some gal to turn on P, you let me set it up."

Fritz was not happy, but at least the two weren't laughing anymore. "No way, you do as I tell you or get out," Fritz demanded.

"Okay, just for shits and grins, what's your plan, Fritz?" ZJ knew that this was going to be good, as Fritz wasn't thinking with his head anymore.

"You two tell P that you have work to make up, and that you need him to stay after school and help you. I'll send in Charlotte to see you two. When P isn't thinking, you ask to go to the can, and you and LD just leave the room. Charlotte will tear her blouse and scream. I'll come in to witness the whole thing, and we'll have him." Fritz was a bit lame at this. The two weren't impressed at all.

"Why the hell would Charlotte do that? LD was amused, but he was still probing.

She's a big jock in school," LD continued. "She's a good girl and everyone knows it. How do you get her to set up P? This is another loser plan, just like last time. Charlotte don't owe you enough to do this. This is doomed before it starts."

"I tell you, she doesn't need to be expelled," Fritz stated.

"What? She's not going to get expelled. She's an athlete and a good student," LD was really curious now.

"You can believe me," Fritz was sure of himself.

"Sure I can, you liar," ZJ was baiting him again.

"I own her," Fritz was bragging.

"Yeah, sure you do," LD taunted him.

"I do," Fritz was sounding like a child, not a fifty-plus adult.

"How?" ZJ baited him.

"She got drunk and got laid at a hockey game. Well, more like raped, but who cares. She went to

Nancy. She was also in possession of some weed, and you guys probably sold it to her." They had. Fritz was bragging again.

LD was on this one like a duck on a June bug, "Fritz, you getting into her pants? Because if you're banging her, she'll turn on you."

"I'm not banging her! God! You two are sick." Fritz didn't want to go there, and the two sensed it.

"You better not be, Fritz," LD was scolding him.

ZJ was growing bored with this game. He looked at LD but didn't say a word. LD knew that they now had enough to get Fritz into deep trouble.

"We'll be back to you with a better plan than this, and you can sure as hell leave Charlotte out of it. In fact, our plan will nail P for good," ZJ was bragging now.

ZJ and LD walked out into the hall of Northwest High, gave each other a high five, and then ZJ dialed Big Guy. When he answered, all ZJ said was, "Got him."

The phone went dead as Big Guy hung up. Big Guy looked out the window of his apartment and said under his breath, "Got Ya."

Chapter 28

A Walk in the Parking Lot

Big Guy looked at ZJ, walked around the front of the glass coffee table in his living room, and said, "Just kill P." He delivered that line as if he had only said, "Get me a soft drink from the refrigerator."

ZJ's breath was taken away, and he asked, "What you mean is, off P, right?"

"Yeah."

"Hold on, Big Guy, we sell dope; we don't do death."

"Wanna bet? You'll do as you're told, or I'll have you killed. The boys upstairs want this done *their way*." Big Guy had just delivered a life sentence.

ZJ and LD were both sober enough to realize that an act as despicable as this would seal their fate forever. They would never be able to escape such an act of pure evil.

Big Guy began to elaborate on the plan, "You don't have to be a brain surgeon to get this figured out. Hell, get high if you have to, but I want both of you to do this. I want you to solve Fritz's problem, forever. He can't get it right on his own. We have enough on tape to implicate him after P is dead. We'll send the tapes to the cops if we have to. You two will have to fill in the blanks for the cops, but I'll help you through that," Big Guy had it all figured out.

"It'll be great training for your future. I want to remind you that you have no choice in this. You lost your choices a long time ago; now it's time to pay the tab."

"I don't want anything to do with this," LD was very clear about this. He was also very scared.

Big Guy went over to the coffee table, opened a small drawer under its surface, and pulled out a .22 semi-automatic. Very dramatically, he grabbed the back of LD's hair and put the muzzle of the gun to LD's temple. LD could feel the cold steel pressing against his temple, and he knew that Big Guy wasn't playing.

ZJ got his act together at this point and focused on the event that was taking place. He knew, full well, that Big Guy would pull the trigger as much as take his next breath. Big Guy had just demonstrated how cold he was, and ZJ was getting the main idea of the lesson. "Look, Big Guy, I'll take LD with me. I'll see to it that he does as he should. Now, let's just put that thing down and get on with business. How do you want us to do this?"

ZJ's play worked, and Big Guy put the .22 with the matte black finish on the coffee table.

Big Guy had listened to the tapes, and he was going to work Fritz but good. This was the opportunity to turn Northwest High into a drug marketplace that would outperform any other high school. The boys upstairs would love this. Once he started blackmailing this principal, he could get his drug reps into the places he wanted them. Plus, he could obtain the school drug counselors' records of past and present users. He could create a client list that would serve as the marketing plan for the entire district.

Big Guy had some instructions for them, "I want you to work with Fritz, but use Brenda instead of the girl he wants to use. We own Brenda, and she'll do exactly what we want. Maybe she can get Fritz in bed. Then we'll really have a lock on the situation. I'll work with Brenda to get Fritz to make a statement to her that makes it appear that Fritz wants P dead. It won't make any difference if he makes a statement to her or not. We'll make one up for her to testify to, anyway. He'll even look as if he went to bed with her, whether he did or not. Statutory rape is enough to lock him up. Appearance is as good as the deed."

"Where do we do P?" ZJ wanted to know.

"We do P at school, after the student/parent conferences. We get LD's mom all worked up and cut her loose on P at the conference. She's sure that her little boy is just misunderstood, and if we get lucky, the outburst will push P into the after conference hours, forcing him to leave the building after everyone else is gone. God, that poor man; his last images on the face of this earth will be LD's mom chewing him out for being so unfair to her baby." Big Guy really thought that was funny.

"You two wait in the parking lot. He always parks at the very end of the parking lot so he can get a little exercise each day. He thinks that he can walk off that fat gut of his. It hasn't worked so far." The boys were paying close attention.

"When he gets to his truck, just walk up to him. He won't suspect a thing when he recognizes you two. I want each of you to put one bullet in his head and cap his ass. Then the gun goes over the side of the Wabasha Bridge and into the deepest part of the river. When you're done, don't come back here; go to Brenda's house and I'll have cookies and milk waiting for you," Big Guy thought he was being funny.

He handed ZJ the .22 semi-automatic. He then

went into the back room, came out with a silencer, and showed it to ZJ. "Use this in the parking lot so there's no noise," Big Guy had said enough.

They left the apartment and had no more than cleared the stoop when LD started talking. Not really to ZJ, but mostly to himself, "I wanted to be bad; I wanted to have sex; I wanted to get wrecked. You, ZJ, you're my best friend, and now what? What? What the hell! You son-of-a bitch! ZJ, what have you gotten me into? Big Guy would have killed me if you hadn't stopped him. We're about to become killers. We're not even eighteen and we're about to become candidates for life without parole. What kind of mess have you gotten me into? We sell dope, but we're minors, so we get probation. We get guys laid, and that ain't even breaking the law. We get high and we get whores, but that don't get us nothing except trouble with our parents, and they'll just say, 'Boys will be boys,' so we had nothing to lose," LD was sounding very worried.

"But if we kill one of the best-liked teachers in school, we'll be tried as adults," LD's voice was now getting louder.

"If we kill a guy who's been married for twenty-eight years, a father of three, and unlike you and me, sober for twenty-eight years, forget the prison sentence —— we are just plain evil. We're about to kill one of the only people in that school who really helps kids like us, and you know it."

He was not about to stop, and ZJ was determined to just let him vent, knowing full well that the two would be dead within the week if they backed out. He just let LD go on.

"He teaches when others just talk about it. He don't lecture at us; he listens to us when others can't wait to get the class over. He bucks the system and goes to the wall for kids. He stands up to Fritz when others are ass-kissers. He's more of a rebel than the two of us put together, and we're supposed to walk up to him because he knows us, trusts us, and he'll let us. Then we're going to stick a gun in his face and cap him. You got it, ZJ? Are you going to do that?" LD was hurting.

"What?" ZJ asked, as he was just ZJ at the moment. Not a killer, just ZJ. LD knew that what they were about to do was just plain wrong.

"ZJ —— 'What'! Is that all you can say, 'What'?" LD was scared to the soul.

"What, LD, what? What do you want?" ZJ yelled.

"I want you to tell me we're going to drive to the nearest police station and tell them everything," LD was serious, and ZJ knew it.

"LD, what are you thinkin'? We work for Big Guy; Big Guy works for somebody who tells him what to do. Big Guy didn't think up this thing on his own. Big Guy is just doin' what he was told to do. Someone workin' the bigger picture is workin' this one. Big Guy, his boss, you, and me are just pawns bein' moved around on the board," ZJ was trying to rationalize having to become a killer.

"This is bigger than just us two," he went on, "and these guys have got it all figured out. They send us, the sales force, into high schools with years of knowledge about what the high schools will tolerate and what they won't. All the mistakes have already been made. All the games have been played before, and these guys are sittin' on years of knowledge that they've gathered throughout the decades in which the "War on Drugs" has been in place. They know where they need to place us in the schools to maximize sales; they have the psychological profile of every user down cold, and they know who the junkies are before they know it themselves." It was obvious that ZJ had been on the streets for most of his life.

"We were taught how to get kids to experiment. The bosses know how to get underage junkies to pitch to the new, younger junkies so we can keep gettin' high. They keep girls bangin' us. The whores keep tellin' us how cool we are so the whores can get high. They own your good-for-nothin' ass, and they will kill you just as much as look at you. You bet your ass that I'm gonna walk up to that holy, holy bastard and shoot his ass off," ZJ was telling him the "Truth" according to ZJ. He was now telling the facts of life as they apply to a junkie caught up in the day-to-day life of use and abuse. "Then, when I'm done, you're gonna take that gun and shoot his ass off, too, because you'll be alive the next day, and that holy, know-it-all motherfucker will be dead." ZJ was acting as if he was as bad as they come. It was bravado. He needed to find the courage to do this thing.

LD was asking himself questions now; he was sucking on a bottle of Old Crow that he'd made ZJ stop to get. He took a long pull on the tea colored liquid and swallowed it as quickly as he could. God, it felt good to just plain get drunk. By the time ZJ pulled up in LD's driveway, LD was absolutely silent, withdrawn in deep concentration. The two LDs in his head were debating. One wanted to run and get help, pay the price, clean up, and live without the constant fear of being caught by the police. This was the LD that had been compromised by Fritz, or worst of all, the one that Big Guy would kill for sport.

Then, there was the smart, manipulating LD, who would look to control this situation and turn it to his advantage. He was totally engaged in this line of thinking when he went to bed. Yeah, he was just like any normal teenager with a drunken dad asleep in front of the TV, and with a mom who was worried sick about the child she had brought into this world. He just got drunk and eventually went to sleep.

Chapter 29

The Deed

The parent/teacher conferences went as expected for me. The parents of the really good students were there in force to receive accolades from not only me but from all of the teachers.

The parents of students that teachers really needed to have contact with never show up at these meetings. This conference was no exception. The kids that the system has given up on are rarely represented at teacher conferences. Worse yet, the number of times that the parents of struggling students have been involuntarily summoned to the school hasn't made going to a school function any more pleasant an experience. Why should they joyfully show up at a parent/teacher night?

The end of the evening was approaching, when a lady who had been standing in the wings with her fidgety husband approached my worktable. We were in the gym at tables with folding chairs. It was late in the evening, and most, if not all, of the parents had already seen me. I was sitting with a former student's mom who was filling me in on the progress of her child at college. The conversation was important to me. I was not paying too much attention to the couple that soon became irritated at the length of the conversation I was presently having.

"I think you've taken enough time," was the first thing I heard from this obviously upset woman. "You know that the evening is over, and I haven't had a chance to talk to you because you seem to take great deal of time with every parent here," the tone was unmistakable; I was in for an emotional tongue-lashing. This overweight, stout woman and her unshaven, tattooed husband were well on their way to making sure this wasn't an enjoyable experience for me.

"And so I do," I stated as a matter of fact.

"I'm LD's mother," she left no uncertainty in that statement.

"How can I help?" I was half-hoping that I could just listen to her complaints, agree with her, accept responsibility for the child's state, and go home.

"You called LD 'Curly'?" LD's mother's tirade had begun, and I was about to get both barrels for something she had not even been present to see or witness. She did not understand what the name was about. The use of this pet name had been taken out of context. The real problems that this child faced would now be disguised by this swindle of the truth. So what? It wasn't the first time, nor would it be the last, that I took the heat for deep-seated problems.

It all came back to me now; I had indeed called LD "Curly" after he had gotten a new haircut that curled his hair in tight ringlets. I was kidding around, and anyone who knows me knew that I was kidding. It was one of the ways that I got to know tough kids. I would use a kidding manner and lots of winks and nods to soften them up. When LD had shown up with a new haircut, I thought it might be an opportunity to break the ice with him. I thought I might get through that tough, thick skin. He had to laugh at himself, and for a while, I thought that I could get a pet name to stick that we could both kid about.

I guess that if I had it to do over again, as politically incorrect as it was, I would do exactly the same thing.

Believe me, once taken out of context of the moment, and out of context of the conversation, it looked really bad. It took on its own ugliness. It had legs and was now an issue. I had been as self-effacing in that conversation as possible, teaching through example that we could all chuckle at ourselves in a playful spirit.

In the classroom, at that moment, it was as though even LD had bought into it. He ripped me a few times and the contest of wits was on. It was really a lot of fun. The results were that he knew how quick I was, and, also, I knew how quick he was. It all ended in good fun. It was also the end of the "Curly" thing, as I wasn't sure if he had been as good a sport as I'd thought. Now, I was really sure that I had screwed up.

"Do you really think that a teacher should call a kid 'Curly'?" LD's mom was really mad.

"No, Madam, and I'm sorry," I was admitting my wrongdoing, apologizing, and trying desperately to make amends. I didn't know where this was going, but it was looking like I was in for a verbal butt kicking, and I was right.

She went on —— and on —— and on. I just listened, hoping that the storm would pass, but she had someone here who had apologized to her. The torrent of anger was dumped on me. The place was empty except for the three of us. Dr. Fritz was the last to see us, and as long as it was me getting the what-for, he didn't care to interrupt. He just went home.

Finally, I said, "I'm sorry, but I have to teach in the morning, so this has to end."

She just got madder and madder, so I said, "Look,

you can call and make an appointment in the morning." After what seemed like an eternity, she finally gave up. I was sure that the chewing out that I had just received was about more than my mistake of calling her son, "Curly." I was sure that she knew, intuitively, that her son was in trouble. I was the repository of her anger and fear at the moment. He was, after all, her baby. His dad didn't say a word but just sat and fidgeted. I got the feeling that he really wanted to go home.; so did I.

As I was picking up my papers and grades from the table, I remember thinking to myself that I really didn't need this. I was very tired, tired beyond what I should have been. I was also suffering from indigestion, something that doesn't normally happen to me. But boy, did I have an acid stomach. I remember thinking to myself that this was the last time I would eat the free pizza that the PTA provided for the teachers on parent/teacher conference night.

As I finally went out the front door of the high school and into the night air, an attractive young lady stood up from the bench that had been placed next to the flagpole. She couldn't have been more than sixteen. She wasn't dressed like a Northwest student, but was disheveled and had worn clothing, and she approached me.

"P-Daddy, talk to me," it seemed she was talking to me.

I was standing in front of the school in a well-lit area and the security cameras were on. What did I have to worry about? She wasn't a big girl, and as style goes in high school, no one knows what dress means.

"P-Daddy, stay here and talk to me?" She had become insistent and a bit demanding.

"Who are you?" I wasn't feeling well and I really

didn't want to deal with this. I was tired and I had a belly full of tacks.

"I'm Brenda. You don't know me, but I know you." I was surprised at the articulation of her voice. She really seemed to know me. She was talking in a soft, warm tone. "Brenda, I'm tired and I want to go home. I don't feel very well. You can understand that, right?" I was hoping for deferment and empathy.

"Sure, sure, but look, I need to tell you a story. Will you please listen?"

She was now changing her tone, and her face was begging for my attention.

I was feeling even worse, and the pizza I'd had on the run between school and the conferences was really taking its toll on my digestive system. "Look, Brenda, I have had it. I really want to go home. Come back tomorrow and I'll talk to you at school, or maybe after school?"

"Sure, sure, but I think this story is important for you to hear." Again with the pleading.

I thought, *Oh, what the hell?* "Please be quick."

"Well, it starts with a student of yours who was in deep trouble at home and in school. She was like me, a kid off the street, but none of that seemed to matter to you. She wasn't much to look at until she met you —— she cleaned up real nice. In fact, she told me that you were as close to a father as she'd ever had. Doesn't say much for her life, does it?"

I didn't have a clue where this was going.

"Somehow you got to her," she continued, "and she got into AA and cleaned up her act. Maybe you were just willing to listen. Maybe it was the contacts you made for her to get counseling. You knew that none of that would have happened at school. The best that could have happened would have been a counselor that would have given her numbers to call," what she said was all very true.

"They're all scared of Fritz, so they do a half-ass job. They're not paid to do anything but get kids to pass their stupid test so Fritz looks good at the board meetings. We may be dumb, but we're not stupid. I think you cared and she sensed it. I don't know what happened. All I know is, now she has a good chance at a real life and you were part of that solution —— maybe all of it?" Brenda was trying to tell me something without telling me directly.

"She used to tell me that when her parents got drunk, were fighting, and were about to hurt her or each other, she would punch 911 into her phone. Then, all she had to do was hit 'Send.' Let me see your cell, yeah, give me your cell. I'll give it back, I promise," Brenda was insistent.

She took my cell and programmed in 911 on the speed dial. She looked at me strangely. I couldn't get a read on it, but it was definitely strange. "There you go. Everyone should have 911 on their speed dial. All you have to do is hit one and you have emergency on the way, in case you ever need it. Hey, P, be careful, okay?" Again with the veiled speech and body language that was saying, "Just do what I say."

I started to reprogram the phone, when in a stern voice, she said, "Hey, P-Daddy, for once in your life, just do as I ask. It won't hurt you. In fact, just keep that phone in your hand until you get into your truck," she was ordering me now.

"What's going on here?" I demanded.

"Can't tell you, P." Brenda was not going to reveal what she knew.

"Why 911 on the cell, and why should I carry it in my hand?" I was a bit worried now, but also tired and a bit scared by the increasing pain in my abdomen.

"Just do it, please. Just this once, do it for me?" she pleaded.

All I could think to say was, "Okay." I was tired and I wanted to go home. I was sure that tomorrow I could get out of the other kids what I needed to know about Brenda. I told myself this because tomorrow was another day, right?

I turned to go to the parking lot and started walking to my truck, when it occurred to me that I should have gotten more out of her. I should never have walked away without knowing what was going on.

I turned around to see if she was still there, but she was gone, vanished into the night. I thought, *How strange*, but, for some reason, I left the phone in my hand. In fact, I put my finger on 'One' and went on to my truck.

I approached the truck. I opened the door on my small, green Ford Ranger. The night had turned cold and there was a light mist in the air. A voice out of nowhere startled me. Then I saw ZJ and LD standing there looking at me. I could just barely make them out in the mist and the dim light of the parking lot. My chest tightened; it was as if someone had straps on my chest, the kind with ratchets for tightening, and it felt like an invisible hand was cranking down the ratchets so tight that I could not breathe. The pain in my arm and jaw was fierce.

I hit the one on the cell. My stomach was hurting, I was sweating, and I was seeing stars. It was not good and I knew it. I was in trouble, and I felt weak in the knees. I turned to look at the boys, and, *Holy shit!* was all I remember thinking. I think I said it, too, but I'm not sure. I do remember looking at a flat black gun with a silencer on the barrel. It was looking me right in the eye, but that's all I remember, because I then went down and out.

Chapter 30

Letting Go

ZJ walked up to me as I was lying on the ground. He placed the silencer an inch from my head, pulled back the action, and chambered a .22 caliber bullet. He was ready to take his first life and seal his deal with the devil.

From the boy standing next to him came a loud "Don't!"

ZJ stopped for a second and looked LD right in the eye. "What?" ZJ leaned slightly forward and opened his free hand, palm up, in a gesture to LD.

"Don't! He's dying right now. Hell, he's probably dead already. He sure ain't moving. Anyway, he'll die without us. ZJ, don't do it."

"I have to do it, don't you understand?" ZJ was shaking. He stood upright with arms outstretched and moved his arm outward in an open symbol of vulnerability to LD.

"Let me see if there's a pulse, ZJ. Just wait until I see if he's dead already!" LD was moving towards me without waiting for ZJ's approval.

"What?" ZJ had moved out of the way but he was still shaking. He was squeezing the gun so hard that his hand was hurting. It was shaking hard; he was close to losing control of his body.

LD came over to me to see if he could find a pulse.

Those health classes had done him some good; he knew were to look and how to feel for a pulse. He couldn't find any signs of life. He looked up into ZJ's eyes and flatly stated, "He's dead."

Typical ZJ reaction, "What?"

"Holy shit, ZJ! He's dead!" LD was sure. He was positive.

"What?" ZJ was stuck in the moment, standing there, cold, wet, shaking, and ready to do what he came here to do.

"All we have to do is walk away; he's already dead." LD wasn't kidding. LD was begging ZJ, his trusted friend for as far back as a fifteen-year-old can remember.

"You're shittin' me. I'm gonna cap him anyway. It'll make Big Guy happy." ZJ just wasn't thinking. ZJ just didn't think, sometimes. ZJ the actor, the bad guy, had to have LD do the thinking. Fifteen-year-old children don't see these relationships of interdependence on their own. LD did.

"No, no, don't do that. We haven't committed any crimes yet. Let's just go tell Big Guy that Mother Nature beat us to him. We get our money for doing him just the same as if we had capped him," LD was negotiating with ZJ. He was selling hard.

"What?" ZJ was in perfect ZJ form and using his limited vocabulary to describe with the one word, 'What,' all the emotion he could muster.

"Put that gun away, 'cause I'm walking. Let's go before the police get here. He has a cell phone in his hand. Come on, ZJ, the police are on their way right now! Let's get out of here, now!" LD was yelling. He turned his back to ZJ and under his breath said to himself, "For God's sake, please come with me, ZJ."

LD started walking down the parking lot, towards

the dark end. ZJ lingered for a moment, thinking that he should just walk over and pull the trigger a couple of times. The further LD got away, the less sure he was that LD wasn't right. The moment had passed, and so had the passion for killing. The anger had started to calm down. He pulled the action back on the .22 and disarmed the gun, put on the safety, and stuck it in his pants. He let go of the anger, finally, and started walking and then running to catch up to LD.

When ZJ caught up to LD, LD locked eyes with ZJ as only LD could. "ZJ, I'm going to go straight. I'll get clean and sober." He grabbed ZJ with both arms, shook him, and smiled. "You're going to help me. I'm going to help you. I don't know how or when, but we're going to let go of this life. We're going to get right with God and the world. I swear that we will, and you're coming with me." The two ran through the parking lot, just like a couple of six-year-olds. They were laughing and shoving each other, and for just one moment, they were the same two little boys that had started school together.

Chapter 31

Resurrection

They say that your life flashes before your eyes before you die. I must not have been destined to die. There must have been some deed I still needed to do, because like the proverbial cat, I used one of my nine lives up. The only thing that really stands out about what went through my mind at the moment of truth, as I was going down, was the pain and that damned indigestion. I was so hurting that it occurred to me afterwards that ZJ would have done me a favor if he had shot me dead. The pain in my chest was unbearable; it was the worst and scariest thing I have ever experienced.

I was later told by officer Strand that the 911 call was booked at 9:48 P.M. on May 11, 2001. It had not been the 911 call that had started the rescue effort, but had been a female's anonymous call at 9:45 that had started things in motion. The call was short but to the point.

Officer Strand visited with me several weeks later. According to him, the first 911 came in at 9:45. He had the recording and played it for me, *"I'm at the Northwest High parking lot, and it appears that a man is being mugged."*

The cell phone that had been used was a stolen cell, so the caller ID was worthless to the police. The identity of the caller was unknown, except to me. I wasn't asked who it was, so I didn't volunteer anything. I knew who had placed that call and why. I don't know what I would have said if I had been asked about the caller. It doesn't matter; I wasn't asked.

Officer Strand told me that the police arrived at about 9:50 and saw nothing unusual in the parking lot. All that was there was a solitary, green Ranger parked in the furthermost corner of the lot. Because of the call, the officer checked out the truck.

He thought he might have seen a pair of shadows in the distance out on the football field. He might have heard a couple of young guys joking around. Given the fact that he also saw me laying on the ground near the driver's side of the truck, he gave no pursuit. He did call in the need for medical assistance and for backup.

The next one on the scene was a female, a rookie cop who immediately started CPR. She said in her report that I was not breathing and that she could not find a pulse.

Just minutes later the paramedics arrived. The rear doors of the ambulance opened and one of the young paramedics expressed his own shock, as he exclaimed, "Oh, shit! It's P!" Without a second thought, and acting on his own instincts, he grabbed a portable defibrillator. He dramatically cut open my shirt, wired me, and, following the recorded instructions that were coming from the speakers in the machine, he hit the actuator. My body jumped to life. The young lady cop was impressed. She started yelling orders at that point. As excited as she was, she kept her attention on the events that still had to take place to get me to the hospital. The scene could have been written for some TV soap opera. I don't remember any of this; I was later told all of this by Officer Strand.

I was quickly taken to a local hospital with Charlie, the young paramedic, at my side. The whole way, he did as the hospital instructed via radio communication. He was a real professional, and the staff at the hospital had nothing but compliments for him after we arrived. From him, the attending ER Doc got quite a lecture as they wheeled me into an examination room.

Charlie was telling the Doc that I was a special person to him. Since Charlie had gotten me here alive, he expected the Doc to *keep* me alive. The lecture included the short version of how he had been lost in high school, and that this was the guy who had helped him through it. This was the guy who had helped him even when he should have given up on him. Without P, the world would be a different kind of place for him. This guy had saved his life. Now, it was the Doc's turn to return the favor. The Doc was not really listening, but Charlie didn't care. He kept the pressure on to get me stabilized. He pressured until the Doc actually instructed him to leave the ER.

I'm told that my wife and family arrived very soon after the call had gone out to her. My wife is a cardiac nurse with some years of experience. She had called the three children, and if I were the hospital staff, I wouldn't wish this on any staff. The first daughter arrived with her new husband and waited for the other two daughters to get there. The last two showed up and I'm told that the nurse daughter (Daughter number two), the Medical student daughter (Daughter number three), and the teacher (First daughter) circled the wagons and took instructions from their mother. The place was turned upside down in the search for knowledge of my condition. The poor doctor, just trying to do his job, was faced with a barrage of questions that were pointed and knowledgeable.

Long story short, they took me into the cath lab, placed stints, opened up a couple of closed arteries, and I started looking alive again. I don't remember any of this. I was out. I'm also a chicken when it comes to hospitals.

Even though I can't remember, I can share this. I was sure that I wasn't going to die. If I had been meant to die, ZJ would have put a bullet in my head. Thank God that my family didn't know about the attempt on my life by ZJ. It wouldn't have just been the hospital that couldn't wait to get rid of me. I'm sure that if my wife had known about ZJ and LD, we could have alienated the whole metro police association. The kids and wife are not something that you would knowingly take on, as they are quite a force.

I was not what one would call optimistic about my prospects for a long and comfortable life on this parent/teacher conference night. I found myself really depressed. I was no longer in pain, but here I was, a fifty-one-year-old chump with a sick heart and a drug dealer intent on killing me. Worse yet, I was working for an asshole that really wanted to fire me. I was plenty depressed.

I awoke soon after I was brought into my room at the hospital. I cleared the room of all the people except my wife of thirty years. I began to cry. I didn't talk. Unusual for me, as I'm sure my students would say. I just held my wife tightly and cried. I also prayed. I'm not a big believer in organized religion. When I had quit drinking, some twenty-eight years earlier, I had relied on a belief in an organizing force in the universe to help me get through the hard times. Now, faced with my own demise, I found myself praying to that force, that higher power.

I was sure that, for some reason, I had been spared.

The concept of God had lost its abstract construct and had taken on a persona that I don't have words for. All I know is, it wasn't lost in the moment that for some reason I had been given a second chance. I confessed this all to my wife. She just cried through the assurance of her love for me. Over and over again, she said, "I still love you, I will always love you; the kids love you; we all need you, and that's why you're still here. Get it, you big dope?"

ZJ and LD went back to Big Guy's apartment and announced to him that I was dead. Then LD, with total confidence, told Big Guy that they wanted the debt reduced in accordance with the deal that had been made. Big Guy just looked at them without saying a word; he picked up a phone and dialed it.

The conversation was short, "He's dead, according to my people." There was a short silence as Big Guy was smiling and winking at the two junkies. He was sure, at this moment, that the two had crossed over to becoming killers. He really owned them now, for life; he owned their souls. Big Guy was really happy for that one moment in time. He was the ruler of the fate of this pair of young junkies. They were his slaves. He was their god.

Big Guy hung up the phone and dialed a second number; Fritz answered the phone at home. Fritz was drunk. Big Guy paused for a second while savoring the moment, and then stated the facts as he knew them at the time, "This is a friend. P is dead. It was my people who solved your problem. I will be calling on you." The phone was held in Big Guy's hand and the two young junkies could hear Fritz's drunken yelling. The ranting of a fellow junkie, with just a different choice of drug, could be heard all the way across the room. Big Guy owned Fritz's soul as well as the souls of the young junkies. It was a great moment in Big Guy's life; he loved it. "T— tell me wh— who you are, an— and wh— what you wa— want!" Fritz was so drunk he could hardly form the words.

Big Guy hung up, went to the refrigerator, and took out a couple of beers. He handed each one of the young junkies a beer and opened the coffee table drawer. He poured some white powder onto a mirror that he placed in the center of the table. He handed them each a short McDonalds straw and laughed. He started yelling, "Party, party, party, dawgs!"

Just as soon as the last line of cocaine had disappeared, Big Guy's cell rang. It was Brenda.

"Yeah, Brenda, what's up?"

The look on Big Guy's face was one of total disbelief. His mouth hung open, his breathing was shallow, and his face went chalk white. He made eye contact with the two junkies who were sitting in his living room, snorting a thousand dollars worth of cocaine, and asked, "Did you shoot that asshole like I told you?"

"We didn't have to. He was dead when we pulled the gun. He slumped and LD checked for a pulse. He died before our very eyes. He was grabbin' his chest on the way down; he was turnin' white. LD checked, but he had no pulse. He was dead," ZJ was talking as fast as he could.

"Why didn't you shoot him anyway, like I told you?" Big Guy was cool as could be. Both boys wished that he would get mad and let them have his wrath. That didn't happen.

"We weren't going to commit a crime that we didn't have to; he was dead," LD was not going to let Big Guy out of his commitments.

"Well, boys, he ain't dead."

Chapter 32

The Rose

ZJ left Big Guy's apartment stoned on cocaine. LD also left Big Guy's apartment stoned on cocaine. The two were a pair. They both realized that I would ID them. This meant the police, an arrest, definitely parental involvement, but worst of all, it meant drug treatment, either in jail or out. It was the end of the usage. LD was poised on the horns of a dilemma. If Big Guy didn't kill him, his parents would surely end his life as he knew it. Even if he managed to elude the killers, he still had to deal with his addiction. He was in for big trouble, big changes, and lots of heartaches.

LD walked around to the back of ZJ's car and got out a bottle of Canadian Club whiskey. Right there, on the street in front of Big Guy's apartment, he took a good long pull while staring into the trunk. Under the spare tire, the silencer of the .22 was sticking out. LD started to admonish ZJ for not having completely hidden the pistol, when out of nowhere, it hit him like a metro bus, "ZJ, the night we got ripped off, you told me the guy with the hood had a gun with a silencer, right?"

"Yeah," ZJ was acting like LD was nuts.

"What kind of a gun was it, ZJ?" LD had a change of tone.

"A semi-automatic with a silencer. Oh, my God! Shit! I never thought about it till now. Let me see that

.22. I'll never forget that gun." ZJ thought that LD might be on to something.

ZJ reached into the trunk, lifted up the spare tire with one hand, and pulled the gun out with the other.

"Yeah, that's it, LD. How did Big Guy get it? Why would he give it to me to kill P if it was the same gun?" ZJ was putting two and two together, and he was coming up with .22.

LD was way ahead of ZJ; he was always way ahead of ZJ, even though he worshipped him, "ZJ, he wanted us to figure this out."

"What the hell are you sayin', LD?"

"The same thing you're thinking, ZJ. I'm just not afraid to say it. Big Guy set us up for the rip-off and shooting you. He owns us, but we don't really owe the bastard a thing. We never really owed him a cent. Even with P living, we're in so deep he will own us even after the police are done with us. We'll be in debt to him forever."

LD was catching on, "I always wondered why he didn't have us beaten to death when we didn't have the money that night. Now, I know. We're never getting out of this, not ever." LD was starting see the hard reality. The life of a junkie had some real downsides. He also started to realize that he and ZJ had been responsible for the creation of a lot young junkies. This hit him even harder.

LD started chugging the booze. He was really putting it away. He also went silent.

They got into the car and ZJ started for LD's home. As they rode home that night, LD just got drunk. Not unusual for LD, but this was somehow different. ZJ sensed that something was out of place.

ZJ finally broke the silence, "LD, you're gonna feel like shit in the morning."

"No, I'm not," LD shot back in a slurred, angry, yet sad statement.

Not wanting to fight with LD when he was drunk, ZJ let it drop.

LD opened the door of the car in front of his house. He then stood up and straightened his back. He stood in silence with the door open. It seemed like an eternity to a drunken fifteen-year-old child, wise beyond his years and hardened, now, by a life that had started out to be so much fun. As he closed the door, he leaned into the window of ZJ's car, on the passenger side. Looking right at ZJ as he leaned slightly into the window, he said, "ZJ, I don't think we can get out of this one. I think the police will make our lives a living hell. I also believe that what the police don't do, Big Guy will. Big Guy isn't going to let this go."

ZJ just listened as he had done a hundred, maybe a million times before when LD was high. Then the pause; it seemed like hours to ZJ. LD shifted from foot to foot, deep in thought. He was drunk, high, and really messed up.

Finally LD spoke, "ZJ, whatever happens, I want you to know that it's been fun, even when we were just kids, fishing, playing softball, sleepovers, all the things we did before we got mixed up with drugs. How did we get here ZJ?" He paused again, then continued, "I just want to thank you for being a good friend."

ZJ was a bit frightened by LD's tone, but he said nothing. Just another LD rant. He would get over it; he always did.

LD went on, "ZJ, no matter what happens, even if you turn me in to save your own skin, I will not say a word to the cops. You can count on me doing the right thing. You don't have to worry about me. I'll be sober forever. I won't touch any more drugs, ever again."

ZJ was really scared now, but he just started talking, not knowing what else to do, "I never worry about you, LD. You know how to keep your mouth shut. You got my back; I got yours."

"Right." LD wasn't even listening.

"LD, You gonna to be okay?"

"No," LD was serious.

"You mean that? You think you should stay at my house? You're gonna be really strung out in the mornin'; you're gonna be sick as hell," ZJ sounded like he knew the routine.

"No, I'm going to take care of myself." LD turned to the walkway to the, suburban, affluent home that he had been raised in. He had wealth that most in the world would have killed for. He looked at ZJ, and in an almost whimsical way, just on the edge of earshot, he asked, "ZJ, you ever heard the song 'The Rose'?"

ZJ looked at him and replied, "No."

"Well, you should. I really like it," LD commented.

Something was wrong, but ZJ was stoned and wanted to go home. All he could think of was, *What the hell was that all about?*

LD was walking to the house, and, in a low voice, was singing the line, "The seed that lies beneath the snow." Like a lot of drunks, he was obsessed with that one line.

LD walked into the house, so ZJ drove off. As LD opened the door, there was his dad, drunk and sleeping in front of the TV with some TV evangelist talking about the gospel. LD looked at his dad and said, "The apple don't fall far from the tree, huh, Dad?"

His dad never heard a word. His mom was exhausted from fighting with his old man over making excuses for LD and his irresponsibility. She had also fought with him about his drinking, many times, but she'd also always done what she thought she needed to do to keep the family together.

She had collapsed that night on the bed and had gone to sleep just like she did every night. LD was the final thing on her mind before she went to sleep, because she was worried about his unexplainable behavior. She would get to the problem of the bad grades tomorrow, that threatened to keep him from graduating, if she could find the time.

LD went to his parents' bedroom door and put his head against the door. In a very soft voice, and in words that were extremely foreign to him, words that he had not spoken in years, he started to talk to his mom, "Mom, I love you. I don't know how I got here, but I always meant to get right with the world. I always meant to get right with you. Mom, I love you... and I'm sorry. I just don't know what to do," LD was saying goodbye.

His mom thought she heard something, but she was sure she was dreaming and went back to sleep.

LD went to his dad's liquor cabinet and got a half-full bottle of Four Roses. He took a big slug as he walked to the kitchen and got his dad's extra car keys out of the drawer. LD went into the garage and closed the door to the house. He turned the key in the ignition to start the car, but the damned thing wouldn't start the first time. The engine needed work like a lot of things in this house. His dad stirred a little in his chair in front of the TV but shrugged it off as nothing. The engine caught and was running. All the doors and windows were shut to the garage.

I'll spare you the last moments of this child's life, as there is nothing to be learned from his death.

The call came in to the police at 6:30 A.M., just as Charlie the paramedic was counting the minutes until the end of his shift at 7:00. He had heard the 911 call, and in a soft voice had said a few words to God on the way to the call. LD might have been a few years younger than him, but Charlie knew his family from school and didn't want to find what he knew he was going to find. He asked for strength and for a miracle. He got neither. This one got to him. Children always did, especially suicides.

They arrived at the house with the flashing lights and the siren on. LD was lying in the driveway and a neighbor was doing CPR. She worked as a nurse at a local hospital and she was doing what she had been taught, knowing full well that she was wasting her efforts.

LD's mother was hysterical, screaming, crying, and shifting from collapse to standing upright. She was yelling at God, and she was yelling at her husband who had found the boy. She was in shock and was mad as hell. She was in total denial.

The young paramedic walked up to the nurse working on the lifeless child. He had seen death before and his intuition told him that this was a lost cause. He went through the motions, following the instructions being barked at him over the radio by the ER doctors. It was over; this child had been dead for at least two hours.

They put the body into the Ambulance and told the nurse that had worked so heroically on LD that if she wanted to help, she should take LD's mom to the hospital. The doctors would declare him dead at the hospital. LD's mom would need somebody with her. His dad was still drunk. The cops wouldn't let him drive. This was quite a scene. His dad had a dead son, but the argument with the police was about him.

LD's mom and the lady next door, no longer a nurse, just a lady who lived next door, were met at the ER door by the charge nurse. No matter how many times she had done this, it was always the same for her. There is no gentle way to tell a mother that her child is dead. The words just plain don't exist in our language.

Like all the other things that LD had done in his life, he had left his final debt to humanity. Leaving this world in debt was his style. He had a social obligation to grow up, and he'd had an obligation to contribute to this world. His gifts and talents would never even be known. Even worse, he would never fulfill his obligation to make the world a little less profane. He was in debt to everyone, and like everything else he had done in life, he now exaggerated that debt in his death. Now, he had left a mess financially, emotionally, morally, and physically that we all had to clean up.

LD's death took ZJ by surprise. He was in total denial about it, not something unusual for ZJ. He did get it, finally, on the second day after LD's death. He was in bad shape. Even he could not believe the depth of emotion that he felt. It was bad —— really bad. Worse yet, he could not discharge his feelings. He was feeling this emotional storm. He could not get rid of the feelings. He was in bad shape and surprise; LD was not there to share this with him. LD had been the only family that ZJ had ever known.

Chapter 33

Goal

ZJ didn't have a relationship with his family. His dad was in jail and his mom was working all the time to keep the family eating. His older brother was in trouble most of the time. He had learned the family business from his dad and brother, drug peddling. How else would he have met Big Guy at such an early age? LD was ZJ's family and now he was dead. All the conning, planning, and scamming in the world would not and could not bring LD back. ZJ was hurting, bad. He was angry. He was just plain out of control without his partner to do the thinking. He was also addicted. The disease now took over totally. There was no ZJ left, just a disease that had grown like a fast-growing cancer. ZJ didn't have any idea how to get well.

ZJ went looking for his answers in the only way he knew how. Getting high was his first priority. This was his only way to deal with the loss and the hurt. ZJ had gone looking for help in the form of a fix. Without Big Guy to supply him, it was a tough world. He really believed that he couldn't go to Big Guy, because it was Big Guy who'd ordered him shot at the hockey arena. He was done with that relationship unless he could scam or hurt Big Guy. Without LD to watch his back and do the thinking, Big Guy would be a force to be reckoned with. ZJ was right about that one.

ZJ reasoned that he knew two things about life. First, life was miserable without drugs, and, second, it took money to get drugs. He wasn't in any mood to do without either one. The worst part was that LD was gone. He had left a huge hole in ZJ's being, so, to keep the shame, guilt, and hurt at bay, he would get what he needed. Getting clean and sober crossed his mind, but LD was not there to help, so, what the hell, he would live life as usual. He thought about talking to his brother, but he had troubles of his own. Mom was out of the picture, altogether; she was selling and using, same as him.

ZJ went back to things he and LD had been successful at as young boys, back when they had just begun in the drug business. Ripping cars in parking lots had always worked for fast cash. He could steal things out of cars and it was a fast way to get cash. It was something he knew how to do, and it didn't require Big Guy.

ZJ went to the hockey arena, to the parking lot closest to the rear entrance. He and LD had done well here in years past, as sometimes, foolish people put their wallets in the glove box when they went to shoot pucks. A broken window and thirty seconds could yield enough cash to get high. ZJ was strung out and desperate to get a fix. His body was beginning to detoxify.

That wasn't pretty. He was sick to his stomach and had the sweats and shakes; his mind was playing tricks on him. He was willing to do what had to be done.

ZJ parked his car on a street adjacent to the parking lot and then walked to the part of the lot that was closest to the rear entrance. He began his search for the best car for a smash and grab. He was alone and vulnerable without LD on the look out. He was going to get this done, regardless of the risk. He was getting strung-out and sick, and he needed to fix his problem. The final decisions had always been up to LD. This was not as easy as he remembered.

As he approached the end of the parking lot, nearest the rear entrance, he spotted Hank. Hockey Hank, from my class, had been at the hockey arena and was just leaving. ZJ remembered that Hank had been an easy mark in middle School. He could be bullied back in those days with little or no effort. ZJ knew that Hank was vulnerable and alone, this time. There were no friends around at this time of day. ZJ knew how he was going to get well.

"Hank, ZJ here."

"What do you want?" Hank wasn't scared this time and harbored a real dislike for ZJ from years gone past.

"I think me and you are gonna be friends," ZJ said as he approached Hank who was walking towards his car.

"I don't think so," Hank said with confidence.

"Yeah, we are, Hank." ZJ came closer and closer to Hank's car.

Hank went about his business, paying no attention to ZJ or his proximity to his person. Hank opened the door to his two door, 1966 Mustang, leaned the driver's seat forward, and placed his hockey stick and bag behind the seat.

Hank and his dad had painstakingly restored the 1966 Mustang. It was his pride and joy. I had seen pictures of the restoration process. I had been impressed by the attention to detail that Hank had displayed as he put his heart and soul into that car. He had approached this project with total abandon. He loved that car and all it represented in his life. It was a success, one of the few he could display to the world.

ZJ had positioned himself on the passenger side of the car, opposite from Hank. The red Mustang glistened and was spotless, inside and out. This was a true reflection of the care that had been taken to build this car. With the car between them, ZJ made the demand that would make him well, "Hank, if you wanna buy some good stuff, I'll arrange for you to get the best," ZJ was being sarcastic; he knew Hank didn't use.

"Hey, just get out of here. I'm not afraid of you." Hank was not kidding; he really wasn't afraid.

"Well, you should be," ZJ was still confident that this would work exactly as wanted.

"Well, I'm not the person you think I am. I'm not that kid you knew in middle school. I know what happened to LD, and I know why," Hank shot back.

"How the hell do you know?" ZJ was really pissed and was close to the edge of his emotional limits. This was sore stuff that ZJ didn't need to think about.

"Brenda told me," Hank replied.

"How the hell does she know?" ZJ was getting really emotional; just the mention of his lost friend all but brought him to tears. He certainly couldn't share his grief with a kid he was about to shakedown for drug money.

He should have. He would have been surprised.

"She knows all. She also told me that Big Guy sent you and LD to kill P. She and Brit are tighter than you think. She ain't doing that stuff for Big Guy anymore. Brit and I are helping her get her life straightened out."

ZJ didn't care, but he should have. "Well, well, well, ain't we the little do-gooders," ZJ was as mocking as he could be.

"I told you before that I'm not that person you knew in middle school," Hank wasn't going to budge no matter what ZJ wanted. He was going to stand his ground.

ZJ was mad now. Not thinking at all, it was time to milk this sucker and move on, "Hey, Hank, see this key?" ZJ held up a car key he had pulled out of his pocket.

"Yeah, and if you touch my car, I'll kill you," this was not bravado, but ZJ didn't recognize the threat as real. Hank was still just a little pushover from middle school in ZJ's mind.

"You and what army?" ZJ took the key and placed it against the roof of the Mustang. "You can get me some dough, or you can get Macco," ZJ was laughing.

"Don't do that; don't do that, ZJ," Hank was giving him an order.

ZJ opened the passenger-side door while stepping up onto the rocker panel and leaning over as far as he could. He touched the key to the surface of the roof, looked Hank right in the eye, and challenged, "Okay, stop me, pay me, or pay the body shop." ZJ was going to key the car, no matter what, and still mug Hank since he saw him as a wimp. As soon as Hank stepped over to his side, he would hit him with the car door and punch him. ZJ figured that Hank had to have some money on him. He could take anything of value once Hank was down. He would kill him if he had to. ZJ just wasn't thinking.

As ZJ was about to start the key on its journey down the roof of the Mustang, a figure stepped into ZJ's sight. It was Deja vu, all over again; this was someone ZJ recognized. From the sweatshirt's hood came these words, "ZJ, you and I are going to your car, and we're going for a ride."

ZJ couldn't see a gun but he knew one was there. Now, he had a problem.

ZJ was distracted just long enough for Hank to reach behind the seat and grab for the hockey stick. For ZJ, the next couple of seconds were in slow motion, but for the hooded guy, it happened in just a split second.

Hank, in one fluid motion, had pulled the hockey stick from the back of the car, gripped it with both hands, choked up short on the handle, and in a split second had struck ZJ, mid ear, with a force that was devastating. ZJ was dead in an instant, with blood and bone everywhere. The fiberglass-coated blade had done its work with extraordinary precision for such a blunt tool. The mess was indescribable, and no more needs to be said, I assure you.

This was not a scene that the hooded man was going to stick around for. He *did* know that if Hank had done this in a premeditated way, he would not have done it in front of a witness. He knew Hank was jail-bound. He ran like hell for about twenty feet and stopped dead in his tracks. He turned and took out his weapon, a 9mm Glock automatic. He walked back to the car, looked at Hank, and said, "This was in his hand."

He showed Hank the pistol, then, he put it in ZJ's limp hand and wrapped the dead fingers around the gun. The gun dropped the two or so inches to the pavement.

Hank knew that the gun hadn't been in ZJ's hand at the time he'd pulled the hockey stick, but he didn't object. He reached into the car, pulled out his bag, and took out his cell phone. "I don't know who you are or why you did what you did, but thanks. Now I'm going to hit 911. You'd better get out of here."

Hank was crying, shaking, and he felt sick to his stomach. He knew ZJ was dead; he couldn't believe what he'd done, but he was going to call the police. He would do what it took to pay the price for this act of violence. He wouldn't allow this hooded guy to get involved. He would take total responsibility. He would, however, let the cards fall as they may where the gun was concerned.

The hooded man looked at Hank and said, "Brenda's my sister." Now, he ran like hell. He really didn't need the police or the questions they would ask.

Hank called 911 and gave the police what they needed through his sobs and tears. He looked at ZJ, then leaned over and tossed his cookies, gagging and crying at the same time. He had never been so emotionally carried to the limit of his very soul, and he did not like what he saw in his heart.

The police were there in seconds. Officer Strand was the first on the scene, and he was immediately sick. This was a hardened cop, a veteran of traffic accidents, but the sight of a young boy with his head severely damaged was too much, even for him. He then got on the radio to call for backup since he saw this as a crime scene.

The ambulance arrived, and Charlie, the only witness to any of the other violence that had come from this chain of events climbed out of it. He was stopped dead in his tracks. He had been at traffic accidents before, but he had never seen anything as brutal as this. Charlie, the same responder who had saved my life with his quick thinking had arrived at a scene that would be indelibly stamped in his mind. The same guy that was at the death of LD was here to close out the triangle of violence. He walked over to ZJ just as Officer Strand kicked the gun off to the side. He bent over and tried to find a pulse; there wasn't one. He loaded ZJ into the ambulance with all the life support equipment still attached to the young boy's body. Charlie had been the paramedic who had answered the 911 calls on all three acts of violence in those spring days of 2001.

As ZJ was placed in the ambulance, Hank was handcuffed and put in the back of the squad car like a common criminal. Hank ended up in the police station awaiting the arrival of his parents. Hank didn't say a word to anyone; he just followed the instructions of the police. He wasn't talking, because he couldn't, yet.

His parents arrived and it was the first time that he spoke. It was the first time that he felt strong enough to speak. In fact, it was the arrival of his mom and the caring hug she gave him that allowed him the courage to speak.

All that came out was a stare at his father and the words, "Dad, I had to hit him or die." Every question was answered with the very same answer, "I had to hit him or die." The police released him into the custody of his parents, and this little boy, who had acted out his anger and fear, was on his way home.

This little boy, in the privacy of his own home, sat down and cried for a very long time. His mom and dad held him, and they cried, too. Brit soon arrived and cried along with all of them.

He would have to live with the memory of his actions for the rest of his life. He knew that what he had done was excessive, and without justification, but he didn't want to go to jail. What Brenda's brother had done would relieve him of the need to explain his actions to the police. But he had to explain to another person what he had done, because he knew that he had gone over the line. He needed to accept what he had done and tell someone.

I was still in the hospital and was doing well. I was walking the halls still strapped to an I.V. pole. The doctors had kept me over because my wife had talked about the stress that I had been going through at school. It was thought that a few days away from the influence of Dr. Fritz would do wonders for me, mentally and physically. I hated being in the hospital, but it was a lot easier to be at peace with my wife than it was to argue with her. I'll choose peace with my wife over righteous attitudes of correctness, any day of the week.

I was close to the ER when I heard the siren and the buzz of the staff as ZJ's ambulance approached and he was taken into the ER. There was talk of a helicopter and a trip to a class-one trauma center that ended when the doctors saw him. He was declared dead at the hospital. I saw Charlie as he walked into the ER. He had already known what the doctors had just made official. He caught me out of the corner of his eye. "Hi, P," he said, as he walked over to me. He had a huge smile on his face and was genuinely happy to see me up and around.

I responded with a huge smile of my own. I knew that it was his quick thinking and the trusting of his own instincts that had saved my sorry ass. My eyes began to tear up and I fought back the impulse to cry. I couldn't help but think that this young man wouldn't be who he was today if I hadn't been there to tell him that he had value and was important. Dr. Fritz had written him off as a loser, and here he was, more than respectable. A contributor to a greater cause, he was. I also knew that it was because of me that he had graduated from high school. It was because I had lived out my passion in front of a classroom that this bright young man had found his own passion.

"Hey, P, don't you dare cry or I'll start, too. Then we'll have a mess, and we'll have to explain to the others that which is ours and ours alone, got it?" Charlie really got to me. He could do that; it was a talent.

"Oh, I got it, Yo-Yo, but just the same, thanks." I was in tears.

Trying to change the subject, he said to me as proudly as could be, "I'm going back to school again."

"Really, why?" I was glad that he had changed the subject. I could choke back the lump in my throat if I was given a moment to re-focus.

"I'll be attending New York University for ultrasound training," boy, did he sound proud of himself.

"Cool!" was all I could come up with, as I was still fighting the lump in my windpipe.

"I'm going to live right downtown, across from the World Trade Center. Classy, huh?" God, was he happy.

Charlie died on 9/11/01, while trying to rescue people in the World Trade Center.

Chapter 34

Principal Canna, Roll Over

Dr. Fritz returned to making my life miserable for the next year. After that year I transferred to another school, but that's another book.

I found out that Hank was free and had told the whole story to the county attorney. He'd told him everything except about the hooded man. He never did explain the gun. He just shut up, refusing to answer questions when the subject of the gun came up. The county attorney was willing to call this self-defense, but Hank refused to accept the courtesy that had been offered. He pleaded guilty to involuntary manslaughter and was on probation until he was nineteen-years-old, at which time he would be an adult with a sealed juvenile record. He never had to serve any time, as the judge felt that this had been a bad set of circumstances for the boy. Plus, he had supportive parents who had promised that they would get the boy to treatment.

Brenda cleaned up, with Hank and Brit's help. I was part of that, as well, I think? She cleaned up nice.

She had been a graffiti artist in her last life and loved to be known as a "Tagger" on the street. She made for me, in memory of Charlie, a large poster of the Twin Towers on fire with the young man's image transparent and superimposed over the towers. I hang it in my classroom every year. My eyes still tear up every time I look at it. Brenda is in college today and is very politically active. I hope that she is president someday. She should be. The world would be just a little kinder place if she was.

Big Guy is still selling drugs and teaching young people the "Ins and Outs" of the drug trade. He's a teacher, too —— isn't he? The last I heard, he had been given a regional managers job in the organization. Every year he gets better and better at selling drugs. He has the school system down cold and trains the best young dealers in the world. As we spend less on education every year, the classes just keep getting larger; all the better for Big Guy's drug business. His organization is one of the biggest spenders of any cause that politically goes after the public school system. The drug trade just gets better every year, and Big Guy's annual bonus just keeps getting bigger. He still ain't in the Caribbean, though.

Dr. Fritz is still killing teachers. Careers end in his office regularly. He keeps hiring for the meat grinder. He will continue to replace all teachers who show their vulnerability. He just gets better and better at hiring the right kind of teacher, the one he can keep in line and who will never make it to retirement in his school. He loves the numbers. He doesn't care how he gets to the bottom line. Human cost isn't a hard number that can be calculated, so it is not seen or tallied.

Responsibility for creating the drug trade in large high schools is not ever directly linked to the Dr. Fritzs of the world. The aiding and abetting that the school person gives to those in the drug trade isn't even looked at or understood. In that process, it is not what the Dr. Fritzs do, but the sins of omission that allows the drug trade to flourish. Whenever we put two thousand young people in one place for eight hours a day with less than one hundred adults in charge, we're asking the Big Guys of the world to take advantage of us. They do. But as Forrest Gump said, "Stupid is what stupid does."

The teacher's union goes on trying to save teachers, but the Fritzs are winning that battle. Hear me, those of you who are young teachers.

Many of my "Loser" students have gone on to be great successes. Some haven't, but even those who are not setting the world on fire have benefited from having had a teacher that they cared for. That ain't all bad.

One thing is for sure, I tell this story for all those students who want to get clean and sober. I wrote it for ZJ and LD, who in a different set of circumstances might have found a "P" of their own. I know that I have been a positive influence for those who have crossed my path, and I will try, as I get older, to reach as many young addicts as I possibly can. There is, after all, only one of me, so get off your ass and help me, will you? Maybe if Fritz hadn't gotten to LD and ZJ first, I could have helped them. I still believe that I could have. Maybe even you could have.

The best part for me is that despite all the labels, despite the efforts of my mom, now long gone, despite the setbacks, the hurts, the pain, and even the successes, I have but one thing left to say. I hope you're rolling over in your grave, Principal Canna. Too bad I couldn't say it to your face.

Too bad another German schoolman doesn't follow his example.

Printed in the United States
51848LVS00006B/106-129